HOW DID SHE GET THERE

MICHELLE WATSON
BOOK THREE

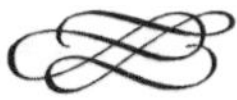

ALEC PECHE

ACKNOWLEDGMENTS

Thanks to Grace Meyer for giving me ideas about this story when my imagination failed me.

Ellen Falk, I swear someday I'll learn grammar. I'm just not sure it will be in this lifetime.

INTRODUCTION

I was in middle school when the first Star Trek series was on TV. There was so much about the show that I loved – but there were two things in particular I was fond of – one was Bones handheld medical scanner and the other was the transporter. So I asked myself at the beginning of this series what would someone do with a special skill like teleportation and how and for whom would they do that job? Michelle Watson was created from that idea. To this day, I wish I could transport myself to anywhere on planet earth in the blink of an eye. Alas, that fantasy only lives in my books.

Sigh,
Alec

CHAPTER 1

After their last case in the heat of Venezuela, Michelle Watson swore she was going to go somewhere cold. It was a mid-September evening, and she was hopeful of seeing the Northern Lights in Iceland. The temperature was about forty degrees as she stepped outside her hotel with her partner, Jason Smith, to look up to the sky.

"Wow, look at those greens. It is like a green rainbow," Jason said.

"Yeah, and the greens are dancing like there is air blowing the colors. It's so amazing and colorful," Michelle said.

They were bundled up in parkas and their backpacks were left behind in the hotel suite. Michelle had researched which hotel would have an outdoor viewing area for the lights. Then she teleported herself and Jason and their backpacks to an area outside the airport. They then took a taxi to their hotel. It was a two-night adventure before they headed back to Langley and their next assignment. They told the hotel they had arrived by a flight from Ireland and fortunately with most countries no longer doing customs stamps, it would not immediately be obvious to the hotel that they hadn't arrived by plane.

During their last case, Michelle discovered a new aspect of her teleportation skill. As long as she wrapped her arm around Jason's head, hugged his torso, and wrapped one leg around both of his, she could move him with her around the world. The two of them were the most valuable agents that the CIA had. The ability to move instantly around the world was a supreme skill for a CIA case officer.

"Did you read up on the lights?" Jason asked.

"I did. The color is from the sun and gasses and cold, and that's all I understand. All I can say is the color is spectacular. I wonder if a plane could fly through the Northern Lights, or are they too high in the sky to do that? Wouldn't that be cool to be on a rocket launched out into space but have the opportunity to go through the Northern Lights on the way out?"

"I think you'll have to be happy with just observing them from the ground. They are like one-hundred-eighty miles in the sky. They don't launch rockets into space here because if you're closer to the equator, then it takes less rocket power because you can use the gravitational pull of the earth to get out in space."

"Wow, where did you learn that?"

"I visited my sister's family last year and took her boys to the Kennedy Space Center. It was one of the facts I learned there. I never knew I would have the opportunity to share that fact with someone else."

Michelle looked at her watch and said, "My research says we should get the best sightings of the lights from eleven tonight to two in the morning. I'd like to find a place to sit and stare at the sky with a thermos of wine to enjoy the view. I think if we had wine in a glass, then the wine would come close to freezing in these temperatures."

"Let's ask the hotel for both items. I'm sure other tourists have asked for the same thing."

He went inside and called the front desk. Michelle could hear the rumble of Jason's voice, but she was soon lost to the colors above. She started when he returned with the items in question. He passed her a folding chair and a thermos.

"They gave us folding chairs so we could bring them back inside as the cold and forecasted snow damages anything left outside."

"I had an Adirondack chair in mind, but I get what the hotel is saying. What kind of wine did you get?"

"I went local. It's bilberry and honey wine. The bilberry is the Icelandic cousin to our blueberry. It's organic and probably sweet."

"Sounds perfect," Michelle said, taking a sip. "It's amazing they can grow anything in this climate. It's delicious. Wow, look at the sky now: the greens are swirling into blues and purples. Maybe the heavens are trying to give us the color of blueberries or bilberries. I think that means that the sun is emitting rays that are crossing through oxygen for the green and nitrogen molecules for the purple or something like that."

Jason smiled and joined her in silently observing the sky. He was thinking of the contrast of being in sweltering Venezuela two days earlier, worried about electricity and water two days earlier, and now here they were sitting in this very cold environment marveling at the night sky. What a contrast in days for him.

His mind drifted to the next assignment they would face after this quick vacation break. One more night of stargazing, then they return to Langley to begin their next assignment. There were rumors that a Chinese pharmaceutical company had plans to destroy an American laboratory that had made significant strides with a cancer treatment. The CIA had no idea where the laboratory was located or who the scientists were who were leading the research, but they were worried.

They continued to watch the night sky and then called it quits once the wine ran out and the cold seeped in with their lack of activity. The next day they would explore the capital city with its restaurants and shops. If it had been summer, they would've liked to hike, but this was a short trip and they would have needed another day in Iceland to get out of the capital and hike its beautiful landscape.

After another day and night, they returned home the way they arrived—Michelle's teleportation service. The next day they had a meeting with Sheila Meeks, their supervisor at the CIA, to be briefed on their new assignment.

CHAPTER 2

"Did you enjoy Iceland and the Northern Lights?" Sheila asked.

"We did," Michelle said. "And the cool fall that is Iceland at this time of year completely pushed out of my mind what the heat and humidity felt like in Venezuela. It was like a weather cleansing."

Sheila smiled and said, "That's a new term—weather cleansing. Well, now, you can forget the weather completely as fall in the United States is pretty good weather as long as I don't send you to one of the peaks in the Colorado Rockies."

"Were your analysts able to find any more information about the company in question?" Jason asked.

"We asked the cancer center at Bethesda to send out an email searching for the company. The trouble is that most of their contacts are clinics, hospitals, or doctors. The laboratory working on this product might be a small biotech company and there are quite a few."

"So how do you propose we narrow down where this might be taking place? From what you've just described, there are hundreds of locations that might host the lab. How did you get word that there was talk of a Chinese pharmaceutical company that was going to target U.S. firms? Did you hear any gossip as to what the lab might be making that was a threat to China? Can you have the health director give you a list of the drugs we pay the most for? That might narrow down the kind of research the lab is doing," Michelle said.

"That's an interesting idea. So many medications or the chemical components that make medicines are sourced in China."

"Could you investigate all Chinese scientists entering the country at the moment? Follow them to see where they're going? I can't imagine there are lots of them entering the United States," Jason said. "Isn't international traffic slowed to some degree as we're exiting the pandemic?"

"Yes, we're looking into that, and the analysts are following up on a few people."

"It feels like we should head back to Iceland as we've got nothing tangible to follow at the moment," Michelle said. "It's weird how the CIA *hears* gossip. How do you know this tidbit or even the Venezuelan gossip was worth following up on? Something is bothering someone in the agency enough that you think it might be true? Or is it hope that someone has actually found a new and significant treatment for cancer?" Michelle said.

"It's probably a little of both. There were a couple of communications that got our attention. Here's our plan: the Oncology Society is having its first in-person seminar in two years. We want you to infiltrate that meeting and place bugs on certain attendees from certain countries. It's in San Francisco, so it's your backyard, Michelle."

"Okay, that's a start. What's our cover story?" Jason asked.

"You'll be a couple of tourists enjoying San Francisco with a room in the same hotel as the conference to give you access to the group. We thought of giving you fake physician or researcher credentials but figured you would only last about one minute if the conversation turns to oncology," Sheila said.

"Okay, how do we identify the people we need to bug?" Michelle asked.

"We'll hack into the hotel and the conference registration, and we'll be able to give you a list of rooms that you'll need to enter in order to place those bugs."

"And then what? It doesn't feel like you are maximizing our skills so far with this assignment. I'm sure you have other agents better at planting bugs than we are."

"True, but we need you to follow up and that's where your skills become invaluable."

"It's not like I'm protesting a stay in San Francisco. It's a great city to work in, but the set-up here seems vague and ineffectual," Michelle said. "I think I'm more suited to rescuing hostages. These mysterious assignments recently from the CIA have me doubting the agency's intelligence."

"I liked being your supervisor better too when you were rescuing people, but you're capable of much more. You saved the world from destruction, and you saved the world from a hideous new street drug. Just run with this concept now and see if it turns into something big, okay?"

"Sorry, you're right. One more question, though. Are we following the right people?"

"What do you mean?" Sheila asked.

"If you wanted to destroy an American lab, would you send scientists, or would you send spies?" Michelle asked.

"She makes a good point," Jason added.

"We're not sure the Chinese know which company is on the verge of a break-through. So, it would seem that they would need to send their scientists first for confirmation, then send in the spies."

"Ah, it's starting to make sense," Michelle said. "I'm ready to head to the city. What hotel is hosting the conference? Should be pretty swanky, and after worrying about food and water for our last assignment, that will be a relief."

"It's a Five Seasons hotel near the Embarcadero," Sheila said. "The Oncology Association conference starts on Wednesday and ends Friday. So, you'll have about four days to verify our intel and if it is true, decide where the biomedical company is located. Your reservation starts tomorrow night as this is Monday. Any questions?"

"No, but can we stop by the lab for equipment?" Jason asked.

"I have an appointment for you in ten minutes."

"Okay, and flight reservations?"

"It's tempting to have you and Jason move around through teleportation, but that creates questions inside the agency. So yes, my assistant has your flight reservations for early tomorrow morning."

"Okay. Thanks, Sheila," Michelle said. They left Sheila's office, first stopping at her assistant's desk for their flight information and then stopping for the equipment on their way home to pack.

They met again in the boarding area of the airport to catch their flight on Tuesday for their journey to San Francisco.

"Is this a boring way to travel now?" Jason asked.

"No, not usually. I can use the time to read up on a mission. Traveling by plane, train, or automobile only annoys me when there are delays."

"Are you going to stop in and see your kids while you're close by?"

"Actually, I told them about my special skill. So I'll check in with them and see what they're up to, and if they have some free time, I'll go. Would you like to join us?

"Sure, but when did you tell them? I was under the impression that you were never going to tell them."

"This may sound weird, but I told them because my first grandchild will make an appearance in about six months and what if that child has magical abilities? I do come from a town full of people with special skills."

"Yes, but it skipped your kids' generation."

"Or maybe it will be latent in my family like it was for me and a special skill will show itself in their future. I needed to prepare them. What if my grandchild arrives with an immediate magical skill? Can you imagine the pediatrician visits trying to fix that?"

"How did it go?"

"I'm the coolest Mom on planet earth and will be the coolest grandmother ever," Michelle said with a big grin.

"So no more 'Mom has a brain injury because she thinks she can teleport' from your kids?"

"No. I also impressed them with the need to keep it a secret. They fully understand that all of the enemies of the United States would hunt me down and kill me given the risk I present to them. They have also been back to San Martin to experience the magical baked goods now that they understand why everything is so much better. It was like they are more connected to the town now that they know its secrets."

"Were they freaked to find out how dangerous your job really is?"

"They were, but I did a demo of how easy it is for me to escape, so then they felt quite proud that their Mom had saved the world from a nuclear bomb, and from a horrible drug in Venezuela, and that I rescued hostages. I think what really excites them is that one day they might have special abilities and the fact I can routinely babysit for them as long as I'm not on a case."

"That's really cool. I'm glad your family knows. They should know about your courage. I'd be happy to join you for a meal if I'm not intruding."

"You won't be."

It turned out that both of Michelle's children had other plans that evening, so meeting Jason would have to wait.

"Have you been to San Francisco?" Michelle asked Jason.

"I've been there before and visited a few sites. I haven't crossed the Golden Gate, been to Muir Woods, or taken a tour of Alcatraz.

It's an amazingly hilly city. I also haven't been to Napa Valley as my wine palate isn't that refined."

"Have you had any cases in this location?"

"No. I mostly go out of the country over a case. The FBI doesn't like the CIA working inside the United States, and it's not our mission."

"Have you sailed San Francisco Bay?"

"No, but maybe I'll look into that while I'm there. It would be perfect if this group has an excursion out on the water. I can enjoy the water and be a spy at the same time."

"I've been on the ferry to Alcatraz, and I've ridden a bicycle across the Golden Gate Bridge and then taken the ferry back from Tiburon. Fortunately, for both crossings, the bay did not feature big waves."

"The bike ride sounds fun. Let's check the program for this convention. Maybe they'll list their organized activities. Somehow, though, I don't think a bike ride to Tiburon is on the schedule."

"No, probably not," Michelle agreed. "Any thoughts on how we're going to find this company that's a target?"

"I plan to read our prep materials. Hopefully, they explain what type of cancer breakthrough we're looking for and that will limit our search."

They spent the next hour reading materials that were so filled with technical medical jargon that it was hard for them to understand.

"This is the second mission for which I wished I had paid better attention to biology in school. Geez, I had to re-read everything like five times to understand how cancer treatment works and what a lab might be up to," Michelle said.

"I have to agree there. I'm thinking that we're looking for something that is called a 'radiopharmaceutical.' It's a combination of something that is radioactive and something that is a lab-made drug. My brain aches just thinking about inventing something so complex. I feel like I have a 1980s laptop for a brain, and it takes IBM's Watson to design something like this compound."

"Yeah, I have to agree. Also, I don't speak Chinese, so just hearing a foreign spy talking means squat to me. Both the American company and the Chinese spies might not even be at this meeting. You would think that if the CIA has heard about a miracle cancer treatment being in jeopardy, then this convention would also be whispering about it. I'm not really good with undercover work, so trying to listen intently while not looking like I'm listening intently can be a real problem."

"Let's hope some of these listening devices prove fruitful and whoever has the task of listening to them all back at Langley hears something we can follow up on," Jason said. He'd been on many undercover assignments for the agency and was better at being invisible yet listening to people. Her background was as an officer on patrol, so she was used to walking around looking for crime. She never did any undercover work for her former police department.

"I'd bug all the rooms, but our briefing materials said there are over five hundred attendees and even if I had that many devices, I would think it would drive Langley nuts with that quantity of worthless conversations. Besides, can you imagine how many languages are spoken at an event like this? They would have to get translators just to figure out it wasn't an important conversation. I'll save HQ the pain of all of that."

By the time they reached the San Francisco airport, they had studied all of their materials multiple times and worked out a game plan. Their strategy was mostly along the lines of fake it till you make it.

CHAPTER 3

They checked into their hotel and then visited the convention area to see if there were any new announcements that weren't in the original packet that the CIA had provided them. Indeed, it seemed that there were tickets still available for a dinner dance cruise one night and a daytime cruise to Alcatraz for significant others of the people attending the convention. They got the information about the boats for both cruises and then walked down to the piers to check out the boats that would be used. Under different circumstances, they would've just purchased tickets for these two cruises, but they didn't have the convention credentials to do so. So, the backup plan was for Michelle to teleport the two of them to a safe location aboard the boats.

They watched one of the boats moving away from the pier toward Alcatraz Island and looked at where people were standing on the boat as it moved in reverse. Using binoculars, Jason examined the different levels of the boat.

"I suppose I could teleport us inside one of the bathrooms, but that could be extremely awkward if it's in use," Michelle said with a grin.

"I think in the case of Alcatraz, we should avoid the boat and go straight to the island."

"Good idea, Jason. Since it's operated by the Park Service, I think I'll wait until they're distracted by an arriving boat and then I'll pop over there now to find a place for both of us to land tomorrow. We'll miss any conversations aboard the boat, but with the wind noise, it's not the best place to try and eavesdrop."

The boat trip was a brief fifteen minutes, and so a short time later, Michelle looked for a place to teleport from and then shrugged her shoulders and disappeared. There were a lot of tourists in the area and they might rapidly blink at the fact that she had been standing there just seconds ago, but then they would decide in their minds that she had just been a mirage. She stood in the shadow of trees near the docks watching people disembark from the ferry. The tour of Alcatraz allowed you to spend as much time as you wanted on the island, so you didn't necessarily return on the same boat you arrived on. She assessed the people who worked on the island and decided that the spot she was in was a good place to teleport to with Jason the next day. As long as they walked around with cameras in their hands, they would look like they were just tourists going off the beaten path to get photos.

She texted Jason,

All clear?

Yes.

A second later she was leaning against the railing standing next to Jason. "I found a good place for us to teleport to tomorrow. I think as long as we walk out of the trees holding cell phones in our hands, it will look like we were getting an unusual photograph. We can take the ferry back here as they are not checking tickets to get back on board the boat. They're not providing transportation to the pier as it's only about a three-block walk, so I don't believe they've reserved a private boat for this group. It appears they just arranged a time."

"Sounds like a plan. We're going to have to be a little more devious on the dinner cruise. The first thing we need to figure out is whether this is a pre-ordered meal or a buffet." Jason said.

"We could board the boat and hang around until everyone sits down to eat, then exit the boat and return perhaps an hour later. Or if we decide there's nothing worth listening to on the boat, when everyone sits down to eat, we'll just leave permanently."

They strolled further down the waterfront looking for the boat that would be used for the dinner cruise. They found it parked in a marina, consisting mostly of fishing boats, adjacent to Fisherman's Wharf. They watched the boat for a while and decided it was deserted, so Michelle teleported inside what looked to be a dining area and quickly explored the ship. Based on the design, she determined it was a buffet meal, so they would have an easier time staying aboard if they decided to do that. Michelle found a utility closet into which she could teleport the two of them on the evening of the cruise. She returned to Jason's side once she made sure the coast was clear. She explained her plan to get them aboard the dinner cruise.

"I wouldn't think the Chinese spies would be aboard the dinner cruise. I don't know why I feel that way, I just do," Jason said. "If the drug company is located in this region, I can't imagine they would join the boat cruise as that doesn't seem like a local thing to do."

"I think it's more important to identify who the company is with the lab that might be close to a major breakthrough for a cancer care. At least if we know who they are, we can provide them with protection. Knowing who the Chinese spies are is important, but as neither of us speaks Chinese, it may be difficult for us to even figure out who is a legitimate Chinese physician attending this conference and who is a spy."

"I would think any physician attending this conference would be bilingual. How else would you understand any of the presenta-tions or talk to your fellow colleagues in this field? So maybe the Chinese spies don't speak English."

Jason took a moment to think back to the various missions he'd had with the CIA. "I was going to say that the spies also have to speak English, but as I think back to all the places I've been sent to by the CIA, I didn't always speak the language of that country."

"Does the CIA have a detector for Chinese technology?" Michelle suggested, trying to figure out how they would identify if any Chinese spies were in their vicinity.

"It probably wouldn't work. Most of our smartphones are made in China, so any kind of detector would be going off about every two seconds."

"That's true. Is there such a detector for sourcing out Chinese telecom SIM cards? That certainly would limit our numbers of people to watch."

"That's not a bad idea. Let's check the question out on an internet search and then message Sheila and have her run it by her technology people."

They each did a search looking for ways to track SIM cards.

"It sounds like it's doable. If they have such a detector, they need to overnight it to us here. The day will certainly become more interesting if we're wearing an earpiece that rings a bell any time we come near a Chinese telecom SIM card," Michelle said, watching Jason type a message to Sheila. "Okay, what else should we do today? We've surveyed the convention center and the two boats being used for the cruises. Should we sit in the lobby and watch people or plant a few listening devices in public spaces?"

"Let's watch people in the lobby to see if that gives us any ideas," Jason said.

They returned to the hotel and looked around, trying to gauge where the best place to eavesdrop might be. It was a tall hotel and sort of a triangle, with a large interior atrium that allowed you to watch an elevator that served all floors including a restaurant on the top. There was a lobby bar with fun seating; however, it was too intimate for eavesdropping. They would need to sit at the bar, or perhaps near the registration or concierge. After a short discussion, Michelle went to the concierge desk while Jason grabbed a seat at the bar. There was no activity worth eavesdropping on, so in an hour they switched with Michelle taking a seat at the bar, while Jason got close to the registration area. After watching the area for a few minutes, he saw his cue. Registrants were selecting their language on the screen in order to check in. Bingo. Now all they needed was a way to monitor who selected the Chinese language. Though to be fair, this was San Francisco, which had a large native Chinese population, but this hotel was not the closest hotel to Chinatown. He hoped that would weed out those Chinese-speaking registrants who were in San Francisco to visit family.

Then Jason thought of another issue—could he see the difference between Chinese and Japanese characters? He did an internet search and decided he couldn't tell the difference given how quickly the screens likely changed and the distance he was from the screen. Rats, so much for that brilliant idea. A new strategy was needed. He decided to watch people meet each other. Maybe he could tell by handshake and conversations if two people were professional colleagues.

After pursuing that strategy, he decided he was again wasting his time. They needed to wait until the next day when people would be walking around with the convention badges that were a sure giveaway as to being a convention attendee. He walked over to the bar to see if Michelle was having any better luck. He noticed that she was talking to someone and decided to take a different empty seat in hopes of her making a critical connection. She gave the briefest of signals that she was aware of Jason's arrival, but then she continued to talk to the woman on the stool next to her. Jason ordered a drink and checked his phone while keeping an ear out for any interesting conversations going on around him.

Michelle's conversation continued for another thirty minutes until someone else walked up to the woman. She stood up, smiled, said something, and then departed. Michelle looked around the bar as if she was searching for a friend, then shrugged her shoulders and left, leaving cash for her bar bill. Jason thought, "This is intriguing." He gave her five minutes and then left and went up the elevator to his hotel room.

He checked to see if anyone was watching him enter the hotel room, but it was hard to tell as this hotel's hallways were open to the atrium, so who knew who was looking at him. He closed the door and then went to the connecting door and tapped.

Michelle opened the door and he said, "What was that about in the bar? Who was that woman?"

"We got lucky! She's the one we're searching for—she works for the lab on the verge of a game-changing breakthrough. She was talking about how excited they are to be presenting here. I have their presentation time so we can learn who the entire team is supporting this lab company."

"Are they based here in California?" Jason asked, thinking about trying to protect a company.

"They have labs near the campuses of Harvard, Stanford, and MD Anderson in Houston. So that narrows things down to just three locations, but the CIA will need someone to understand their research process, as I sure don't."

"When is the company's presentation?"

"It's the general session on the second day of the conference at nine in the morning. Perhaps the CIA can get a physician here who will understand what they are talking about."

"That is if the presenters make it alive to the presentation. It seems that if a Chinese company wants to stop this research lab from developing a process that will revolutionize cancer care and hurt their profits, then they need to stop that lecture, stop those researchers and the company they work for. We need to talk to Sheila. Maybe she can get our resident hacker, Madison Hank, to find the hotel rooms where the company staff people are residing."

"That sounds like an excellent idea," Michelle said as she punched the buttons for Sheila's number.

"What have you found in San Francisco? You've only been there a few hours, and you already have something to report? I'm impressed."

"As you should be," Jason said and added cheekily. "We're the best Case Officer pair that you have."

"Yeah. Tell me why you called."

Apparently, she wasn't feeling his line of B.S. at the moment.

"I randomly lucked out and met one of the lab employees at the bar," Michelle said.

"You should have texted me right away," Sheila admonished.

"I'm really slow at this spy stuff. First, I had to get away from the employee once I had all of her information. Then I had to give the high sign to my partner, then I had to wait for his arrival, and all of this took about forty minutes."

"Forty minutes, huh? I guess I shouldn't complain. I'm not sure our spy school graduates do better than that."

"Spy school? In the CIA? I've never heard of that," Jason said, puzzled by the conversation.

"It refers back to a time when Michelle didn't grab fingerprints because she hadn't thought of it because she hadn't been to spy school. The analyst she was working with at the time was shocked by her words."

"Do we have a spy school?" Jason asked, puzzled. "It has been a while since I was a CIA newbie, but I haven't heard that term."

"No, but maybe I'll suggest that to Assistant Director MacDonald the next time I see her since it would help untrained agents like Michelle."

"Alrighty then," Jason said. "We did call you to pass along some information and get directions from you. Michelle learned that this laboratory company has three locations near Harvard, Stanford, and MD Anderson. We were wondering if your ace hacker

Madison Hank could hack into this hotel and tell us which rooms the lab company people are staying in."

"That's a good idea. Let me see if Ms. Hank can do that. However, what are you going to do with that information? It's not like the two of you can protect multiple hotel rooms."

"True, but I would like to know if the Chinese are on to this particular company. Michelle could pop into the room and see if there are any devices inside. We also need more resources here as we think the first step in stopping this American company is to stop them from making a speech about their innovation. Wouldn't you agree?" Jason said.

"When is the speech?" Sheila asked.

"A little more than thirty-six hours from now. It's at nine in the morning two days from now," Michelle said.

"Overall, we're not supposed to be working inside the U.S. I'm going to have to tell my counterpart in the FBI about the situation and have them get local resources for you. I think I can get resources there by tonight and more tomorrow. Let me get working on room numbers and I'll also work on smoothing the waters with the FBI."

"Could we just say to this company and its employees that they need to go into protective custody and not make the speech?" Michelle asked.

"We could and we could be wrong and mess with this company's finances in doing so. Remember, as always, we're acting on unconfirmed intelligence. We don't know the Chinese are involved, or that we even have the right company."

"Yeah, well so far with your last two cases, your intelligence was confirmed, but I understand what you're saying. Give the FBI our contact information," Jason said.

CHAPTER 4

An hour later, Jason and Michelle were in a bar about two blocks from their hotel meeting their FBI counterparts. It was loud, but they could lean across the table and be heard while they were sure no one was listening to them. They all had beers in front of them. They had been briefed by their agency and were planning their strategy. Madison Hank had been able to hack into the hotel's website and they knew that there were six members of the lab company registered in six different rooms, all on the same floor. It was a different floor than Jason and Michelle were on. Michelle had already placed small cameras focused on the doors of the six rooms. Someone in Langley was watching the cameras.

"Are you sure you've got the right company? Aren't there multiple companies at this conference promoting breakthrough cancer treatments?" Nathan Chau asked.

"There are, but this one has a prominent speaking time at the conference, and I spoke with one of its employees. She mentioned that the stock price of this small biotech company increased in value by ten times when they issued a press release of the discovery they'd made and the fact that they were discussing their findings at this conference. Apparently, to be able to speak at this conference is a validation of sorts of your research," Michelle said.

She could tell the two agents were not impressed with Michelle's deductive reasoning. She was tempted to add that she was riding on gut instinct, and she now had a reputation inside the CIA for turning rumors into truth, but she didn't say anything. The agents would help them, and she could leave much unsaid.

Apparently, the agency had convinced the FBI to place two agents at the hotel for a few days to see if anything shook out. However, it was clear that the two thought they were babysitting the agency and it was stepping over its scope by trying to protect American researchers, but the CIA had bilingual agents arriving the next day. The agency should have put Mandarin-speaking agents in place instead of Jason and Michelle, but Sheila apparently concluded that she and Jason had the knack for being at the right place at the right time for a new assignment.

They expected a quiet night and then the next morning they were going to try and get into the convention area. They wanted to stroll the vendor areas and check out the poster boards which displayed the latest research. Perhaps she hadn't targeted the right company and if they didn't get that right, then the poster board area was where they should search next according to the medical consultants in the agency. They didn't have convention identification, though Michelle thought she could likely get the appropriate identification the next evening once everyone left. She would see if they got anywhere in the morning.

Jason and Michelle were in the hotel gym the next morning as they needed to maintain their fitness and it could be a great place to pick up gossip. They had earbuds in their ears, but rather than listening to music or podcasts, they worked like hearing aids and amplified the conversations around them; that way, if someone was discussing something of relevance they could eavesdrop.

They both stayed in different areas of the gym and listened to the highly technical conversations. Michelle frowned at one point with the thought that while the two men she was eavesdropping on were speaking English, she could barely understand what they were saying. She let her brain glaze over and glanced at Jason.

He gave her a look that said come over here and listen, so she picked up a set of barbells and approached where he was working on his biceps and listened.

". . . I heard about the findings of their study a week ago. I'm anxious to hear their talk as it could be revolutionary for our field —right up there with the discovery of penicillin and infectious diseases."

"I haven't heard anything about this company or their research. What makes their findings so revolutionary?"

The other person speaking explained his thoughts and Michelle thought it was like listening to the parents talking in the Charlie Brown cartoon. All she heard was "wah-wah-wah" as their discussion was so technical.

She and Jason stayed near the pair until they left. Michelle followed them out of the gym and over to the elevator bank, planning on returning to her room and Jason would follow a few minutes behind her. The researchers moved on to a discussion of some upcoming change in reimbursement and Michelle was glad to see them get out of her elevator on a floor lower than hers.

Jason knocked soon after on the connecting door.

"That conversation was more confirmation that we're targeting the correct company and the power of that lecture," Jason said. "Let's check in with Sheila and see what she has for us. We have the sunset dinner cruise tonight, so it's going to be a long day."

Before they had the chance to ring Sheila, she called them.

"We've got police activity outside of the rooms that we're watching. The FBI is acting as an intermediary to find out what is going on."

"Crap," Jason and Michelle said at the same time. Then Jason added, "We were just about to call you with the news that this

Thursday lecture is being gossiped about as big news. One person in the hotel gym said that if it proved to be true, it would be like what the discovery of penicillin was to infectious diseases."

"Just a moment," Sheila said, putting them on hold. Michelle and Jason looked at each other, concerned. Michelle hoped the bubbly person in the bar she'd met yesterday wasn't ill or dead.

A moment later she came back on the phone. "It seems that one of the team members couldn't be roused this morning so hotel security and then the police were called. There is a report of a room occupant being dead."

"Any chance that it is a death by natural causes?" Michelle asked.

"I don't know yet other than there's no obvious gun or bloody wounds," Sheila replied. "We'll likely have to wait for the autopsy. Our FBI frenemies are on the scene and will share with us eventually."

"How old and which gender was the person?" Jason asked.

"Male in his mid-40s was assigned that room per our hacker. I don't have information from the scene yet to know if that is who the DB is."

Michelle relaxed marginally. She was sad that a male colleague might be dead and indeed perhaps someone more important to the research project, but she had so liked the woman yesterday— her pride and joy in her company's work was so evident that she didn't want her dead.

"So one down, five to go in the next twenty-four hours," Jason said. "Can your hacker tell us if the company signed up for the dinner cruise this evening?"

"I don't know. I'll ask. I'll text you with updates."

"Has anyone checked in to make sure the other five are all alive? Are they in an area where we can talk to them about their risks? Have we discussed the next steps with the FBI? In theory, protecting these people is their job and we should be focused on the Chinese. I think this death is our signal that they are here and are unhappy with this company's plans," Michelle said.

"Yes, the FBI was a lot more interested and cooperative this morning once they were informed of what's going on. Talk to you later."

Jason and Michelle looked at each other after the abrupt ending of the call.

"Well, I'm going to grab a quick shower as I think we're going to have a busy day in front of us," Jason said. Michelle nodded and did likewise.

She was drying her hair when the first text came through from Sheila.

Confirmed DB male, identity is one of the team that belongs to the biotech company. Meeting with FBI, detectives, and other company representatives in fifteen minutes in your hotel room, Jason.

Jason and Michelle each looked at their rooms and tidied them up, combined both coffee pots into the one hotel room, and gathered up drinks and snacks from the in-room refreshment center. Jason propped the door open slightly and they waited for their attendees.

"I hope none of the Chinese agents are in this hallway to see the FBI and police come to our room. It will blow our cover," Jason said.

"Maybe we should have them haul you away in handcuffs as though you are a terrorist?" Michelle suggested.

"No need to go that far with undercover work," Jason said with a pained smile.

A short time later ten people filed into the room including the woman who had been bubbly at the bar the previous night and was now red-eyed and teary. Introductions were made.

The two police detectives gave the stink-eye to the FBI and CIA representatives, then led the questioning about the dead man and his role in the company and what the others did. Jason followed with questions about their plans for their time in San

Francisco. Michelle could sense bewilderment, grief, and anger on the part of the room's occupants. Sheila liked to hold the agency's missions behind closed lips, but they were going to have to share some information with these people. She and Jason looked at each other and seemed to silently agree that they were going to have to provide a minimal briefing.

"Does the hotel have video of the hallway outside of the company rooms?" Michelle asked.

"It does and we'll let you know if it shows us anything," one of the detectives said.

Michelle didn't reveal that they had cameras focused on the doors and they had already looked at the footage and hadn't discovered anything yet. They hadn't placed cameras on the balconies and it was certainly possible to get into the room that way, if you didn't mind falling to your death if you slipped. Then she thought about the connecting door. Was there one in that room?

"Was there a connecting door to our victim's room?" She hated saying the words *victim* to the dead man's colleagues, but they hadn't had official identification. It seemed silly as it sounded like those colleagues had seen enough to confirm his identity.

"Just a moment," said one of the police detectives as he pulled something up on his phone screen.

"Yes, there was a connecting door that went to a room not occupied by one of his colleagues."

It was something to consider as they developed a plan to keep these people safe. Was it better to keep them together or move them into one location? She and Jason listened to the others discuss a plan for keeping them safe. They had nothing to add as they had no right to operate inside the United States. The safety of the company and its employees would have to be the responsibility of the FBI and local law enforcement. So what could she and Jason work on in terms of any Chinese espionage activity?

CHAPTER 5

They had correctly figured out the target of concern for the CIA, but they hadn't confirmed who wanted the company and its invention killed. Yes, their intelligence said it was the Chinese, but it could be almost any pharmaceutical company with a stake in cancer care. Maybe the CIA analysts could provide them with a complete analysis of who on earth would benefit from seeing this company and its research destroyed. She dropped a text to Sheila with that request.

Shortly their room emptied of people and Jason and Michelle got the chance to discuss their next steps.

"Given the agency's mission, we can't help this company or its people. This is a domestic issue. We need to find these Chinese operatives," Jason said.

"Actually, I asked Sheila to have the analysts give us a list of all the companies that earn large amounts of money for cancer therapies. I know our intel said it was the Chinese, but I think we need to do due diligence before we focus on just one country," Michelle said.

"Our intel hasn't been wrong in the past," Jason argued.

"No, but it hasn't always contained the full story. What if we had stopped our work in Venezuela after we found there wasn't a threat from the Iranians? We would have never learned about the bigger threat of that addictive drug about to hit the U.S. market."

"True. Should we watch these people to see who is watching them until Sheila has some new information?"

"I guess that's as good an idea as anything. I would think that the company's employees wouldn't do much today given the death of their colleague, but maybe they'll attend parts of the convention. Now that we have fake convention IDs we should be able to move freely about the convention."

Michelle had waited until late evening the previous night and teleported into the registration area to make badges for her and Jason. They were identified by fake last names and a nonexistent biotech company from Austria. They had a discussion about their lack of German or accented English and decided to say that while their company was based in Austria, they originated in the United States.

They would start by finding the poster board of the company's results and setting up a small listening device to capture conversations near it. The company didn't have a booth on the convention floor, so there was no reason to visit that area. Once they were near the poster board, Michelle looked around to see if there was a place to put a camera. After the area was closed for the night, she could teleport in and then up to the rafters high above and place another camera to identify anyone who seemed to have a keen interest in the company's research findings. Until then, they were done with any additional progress they could make in the convention itself as far as finding out who wanted to kill the tiny biotech company and its employees. There were simply too many people speaking too many languages for them to randomly hear people of relevance talking.

"We should check one more thing. Does the largest Chinese drug company have a booth here? Maybe if we got photos of the people staffing its booth, we can check them out with the CIA to see if they're spies. That would speed up our identification process," Jason said.

"True. Is it really that easy, though? Somehow, I can't imagine someone standing around with a badge that says, *Hello, my name is Cindy and I'm a spy.*"

"I agree with your thoughts, but maybe we'll be lucky. You were lucky at the bar."

"Yeah, but we usually only have a lucky strike once in an operation," she said, as they entered the room where the vendor booths were located. Some of the vendors were aggressive and tried to lure them into their booths, and in other cases, they were ignored. Michelle looked at a map of the vending area and confirmed that their target American company did not have a booth displaying their research.

"Can we tell if any of these booths are headquartered in China?" Jason asked, when they had reached the end of the first of seven rows.

Michelle looked at the list and replied, "There are a few obvious names, but I think we're stuck wandering. I'll mark this map every time we pass an obvious Chinese company. I'd offer to add a star to any booth where its occupants were speaking Mandarin or Cantonese, but I can't tell the difference among Asian languages."

"Yeah, I'm in the same boat. Perhaps the agency should have sent case officers who speak one of those languages. I'd ask Sheila for that resource, but I think she's trying to be careful with jurisdiction. She seems to be wanting to keep this operation small so as not to upset our partners in the FBI or the local police. She'd prefer we get in and out without those agencies knowing that we're here. Unfortunately, we had to blow our cover here given the jurisdictional issues."

They finished perusing the hall and returned to their hotel rooms with notes about the various vendors that they wanted to research. They noted that the large Chinese pharmaceutical firm did not have a booth at the convention, which was rather curious.

"You would have thought they sponsored a part of the conference or otherwise had a public presence here," Jason said.

"Maybe they were trying not to be obvious. Let's look at last year to see if they were here."

"The conference might have been virtual last year due to the pandemic."

"True . . .," Michelle mumbled as she searched online. "Yes, it was a virtual conference last year, but there was sponsorship provided by our favorite Chinese company."

"Sheila just sent us a text of the largest pharmaceutical companies in terms of cancer drugs for us to evaluate. The largest firms are based in Switzerland. I wonder if we're targeting the correct company? I suppose we need more information like profits. If a drug is affected by the breakthrough of this American firm, but it's not a huge moneymaker, then the motive disappears."

"Yes. We need some more analysis here. Let's ask Sheila for that. I'd also like a better understanding of how this new discovery works. I think we really need to understand what motive is at play here, and we don't have enough information yet."

"So, did we learn anything by wandering among the booths or the convention people?"

"I don't think so. This is almost worse than learning about refining uranium and making nuclear bombs. This cancer science is beyond my brain to comprehend. I think we need to talk strategy with Sheila. With the FBI and PD on the scene, we're not needed for security. Maybe we need to head to Switzerland or China and be closer to the drug firms, though I'm not sure what good we would do there either," Michelle said.

They checked in with Sheila and planned to chat with her in an hour. So while they waited for their call, they brainstormed what their role might be in this situation. Hopefully, the FBI and local police would keep the company members safe as well as their locations around the United States.

"We need to understand what the scientist was doing for the company. Was he killed because he had the most important role in this discovery or was he the easiest to kill? We don't even know how he was killed yet, given there were no obvious wounds. Again, those are questions for the locals. I'm starting to see your view, Michelle—I think we need to head to the headquarters of whatever companies have a motive and see what we can find."

They knocked around a few other ideas until the phone rang with the planned call.

"So, the two of you are not enjoying your time in San Francisco?"

"I love the city," Michelle said, "But I don't see our mission as being here. The very capable local police and FBI can take over protection and investigation. We circulated in the room and placed cameras and listening devices where necessary, but frankly, learning nuclear fusion was easier to understand than how chemotherapy drugs work. So someone may be saying something relevant around me, but unless I hear the words *We need to kill so and so to stop them from releasing their technology*, it's all white noise to me."

"Ditto," Jason added.

"I think you're right. I'm waiting for results from the autopsy as that might lend us a clue as to who was behind the killing. I've got the analysts searching for companies with motives. Why don't the two of you hang out with these convention people during their social activities until we decide where to go next? I'd hate to think that the Swiss are behind anything and if we need to send you to China, it's closer to San Francisco. It's not often that you get to take an on-the-job vacation at the agency's expense."

"Except we're still working, we're just doing it in a beautiful place," Jason said.

"True," Sheila said as she ended the call.

Jason and Michelle looked at each other and then laughed.

"We've been ordered to hang out in the most touristy places here. I won't complain considering that during our recent mission in Venezuela we were worried about having enough water to drink and showers were a fantasy in a muggy climate," Michelle said.

"Yep. Should we head for the bar and become barflies until the sunset cruise tonight? We'll have to drink fake cocktails, or we'll be hammered by the time the cruise rolls around."

"Yeah, ginger-ale for me. I hope the bay is smooth tonight or I'll be tossing my cookies."

"I checked the marine forecast, and it should be smooth sailing. Let's go down to the bar."

The hotel lobby had various niches for them to hang out and listen. They moved from the bar, to tables in the bar, to various seating areas with potted plants. They had thirty minutes until the cruise and agreed the day had been a complete waste. They walked down to the harbor pier where the boat cruise departed from to get ready to teleport. They watched as the boat loaded with convention attendees who arrived by bus. They were wearing dressier clothes than Michelle and Jason, but for the most part they appeared to be the older members of the convention attendees. Still, they looked okay, and Michelle and Jason waited as the boat departed and then they planned to teleport to the empty utility closet. The crew was busy getting the boat under way and the attendees were either out on the front bow or inside where the dining tables were set up. Some people never liked the fresh cold air of a sail around the bay.

"Ready to go?" Michelle asked.

"Yes," Jason looked around to see if anyone was looking at them. Not that it mattered—people simply thought they were seeing things if they were looking at Michelle and Jason and they disappeared.

Milliseconds later, Michelle was unwrapping one leg and her

arms from around Jason as they quickly separated to take stock of where they were inside the closet and more importantly, making sure no one was nearby. They quickly moved beyond the closet into the guest area of the boat, relieved at not being spotted by anyone. It helped that it was a rare clear sunset and San Francisco Bay was shining in all its glory. It transfixed the guests, while the staff were occupied pulling away from the pier area and into open water. They wore their fake badges which listed them as pharmaceutical representatives from a nonexistent company in Ankara, Turkey. It never hurt to have multiple badges, especially as they hadn't spoken with anyone yet. That way they could fake that their English wasn't very good if anyone tried to get into a serious conversation with them.

They moved through the attendees nodding when that seemed like the polite thing to do. They found a no-host bar and grabbed a glass of wine each, then made their way to the crowd outside who were enjoying a brilliant sunset. They both were trying to eavesdrop on conversations but after an hour, they heard nothing of relevance—not even gossip about the death in the hotel that morning.

"Well, should we leave? I think we're wasting our energy here. I'd say that we were wasting our time, but we have time to waste," Michelle said.

"I agree we should leave. We risk our cover being here and since we're not gaining anything, why bother? Do you see anywhere we can teleport from?"

"Let's just go back to the closet, lock the door, get into position, then I'll teleport us back to my hotel room. I'll unlock the closet door just before we go."

"Sounds like a plan," and they headed below and did exactly that.

They were discussing what they could do to help the case when Sheila called. It was nearing midnight back in Virginia. It was a long day for their supervisor.

"I have preliminary results on the autopsy. There was a drug in the victim's bloodstream called ketamine. That points us to China as it had long been a drug of abuse. We're doing more research on potential locations, but we have you on a flight to Beijing tomorrow and we'll figure out where we're assigning you after that."

"Are you sure you want us to fly there? Won't that alert authorities to our presence? Shouldn't we teleport into the country?" Jason said.

"That's a good point. Let me think about that question and see if we can get you some passports that have an entry stamp and a visa. We may make you Venezuelan citizens or something. Just sit tight while we plan on our end."

Jason and Michelle agreed, and the call ended.

"Have you been to China?" Michelle asked.

"No. I'm not an expert on that region at all, how about you?"

"I rescued someone from one of their labor camps, but I might have spent a total of fifteen to twenty minutes there before I turned the woman over to other resources who took her the rest of the way out of the country. Remember, at the time I was doing hostage rescue; I didn't know yet that I could teleport another person with me. I just used my skills to break into locked locations. I'm a little surprised that the agency hasn't circled back to me to do a few rescues as I could do it much quicker now. There must be some risk assessment somewhere that the more people with the knowledge of my skills, the more they could blow my cover."

Jason looked thoughtful and said, "Yes, there's a true danger to you if too many people start talking about your skills. There's the rescued person and then there are their loved ones. If they're a famous hostage, then it's all the more difficult to send you in. Maybe if I was the agency I would send you in with a syringe of knock-out medication and have you teleport the hostage to a secret hospital bed in the depths of Langley. That way the hostage would never know how they got back to the U.S."

"That's a good idea, but someone would have to train me on injections, and they would have to add medical personnel standing by in case of a bad reaction to whatever drug was given by me. The CIA would have a great reputation of secreting people out of hostile territories, and nobody would come up with anything close to the real way it happened. I might have to suggest that to Sheila at some point as I do feel bad about leaving Americans in situations where they are abused or tortured."

"We have time on our hands and nothing to read about yet. I guess we should access the library at the agency and brush up on China. I'm nervous about traveling there as I'm clueless on the language and customs, and in the looks department, we stand out as Caucasians."

Michelle nodded and they began their last-minute cramming session on China. They would be traveling to Guangzhou as it was one of two major pharmaceutical hubs in southeast China.

CHAPTER 6

The next day Michelle was asked to teleport to Virginia and collect a variety of documents. She and Jason had fake names on their passports, an entry stamp for Baiyun Airport in Guangzhou, after a stop in Taipei, a visa that would cover them for thirty days, and a cover story. She teleported Jason and then their luggage. They repacked for the warm fall humidity in southeast China and prepared to teleport to an apartment in Guangzhou that another agent had rented for them. They planned to arrive in the middle of the night as that would be part of their cover as to why they weren't seen entering the building. They checked and found flights arriving to the airport at two, four, and five in the morning, so their story was believable.

Their instructions were to infiltrate the company in question as the buyers of a pharmacy chain in Colombia. They discussed using Venezuela, but the country was too poor to be buying large amounts of drugs from China. The CIA set up a backstory in case the Chinese checked references. The agency also had a second set of documents related to them as a couple on a honeymoon in case they needed to change their story. Michelle left the second set of documents in her condo in Virginia as she didn't want to give the

Chinese the chance to find them. They thought they had everything from clothing to satellite phones. They also had a briefing on their cover story as pharmaceutical negotiators. This part of China was eighteen hours ahead of Virginia, so if they left at nine in the morning, they would arrive the next day at three in the morning. That seemed like a good time to arrive.

Michelle felt like a spy school dropout as she was so uneasy about her fake identity. She felt even worse as she couldn't understand the language around her. It was hard to know who your enemies were when you were clueless as to their intentions. She said as much to Jason once they settled into the apartment.

"I forgot to ask you what exactly spy school is."

"Sheila and I were talking to one of the analysts and I missed collecting a key piece of information, and I said to Sheila, "That must be something they teach you in spy school." The analyst looked at Sheila and asked if the CIA had something called spy school. Sheila just shook her head at my atrocious comment and I think the analyst deducted a few points from my IQ for the comment."

"That's actually a funny comment. At least now I know how to make jokes about it when it comes up in conversation with Sheila. I know that you're uncomfortable here, but remember we were also uncomfortable in Venezuela. Granted, we could speak Spanish and understood what people were saying around us for the most part, but my only piece of advice is don't act overly aware or suspicious or that will make whoever is watching us suspicious. We want to keep a low profile, but I admit it's not easy. I want to snoop around this pharmaceutical company before we try our cover story as buyers for the Colombian pharmacy. Perhaps that surveillance time will give you a little more comfort in this country."

"Surveillance is a good idea. How should we go about it? At the extreme, I could probably teleport inside one of their air vents near the CEO's office so I can eavesdrop. Trouble is, I can't understand what they're saying, but maybe we should consider planting listening devices around this company."

"That's a thought. Langley would be able to have bilingual analysts listen to any conversation for us. Let's search for where we should leave these devices and find some pictures for you so you can safely teleport there in the middle of the night tomorrow," Jason said.

"I left twenty devices in my condo that I can fetch for that purpose tonight. I have a feeling I'm going to conk out sometime today given the time difference. I'm thinking it's 11 o'clock in the morning yesterday when it's actually four in the morning the next day. I'd take a nap but I'm not tired at all. I suppose we should go out and get groceries as doing something routine like that will help allay my unease about being in China. In case you can't tell, I'm rather anxious about all of the surveillance of the average Chinese citizen."

"If it makes you feel any better, I think every agent at the CIA feels the tug between the arrogance of 'I know what I'm doing in this foreign land' and the fear of 'what if I'm caught.' In your case, you can disappear so there should be no real fear. You're safe."

"I am, but you're not safe, so I have to worry for you."

"You know I've been with the agency for nearly thirty years and I've always managed to find my way home eventually. Don't waste any time worrying about me."

"Yeah, that's easy for you to say. When you come from the blue brotherhood, you always worry about your partner. They're family and they are vital to your safety just as you are to theirs. So I can never look at just keeping myself safe; I also have to worry about you. So suck it up," Michelle said with a smile.

"Okay, let's make a list of what we're looking for at the grocery store. Let's take a quick look at the cabinets here just to make sure our contact didn't stock the refrigerator and kitchen."

By daylight they had a plan for the day. They would take care of the necessities like exchanging money, grocery shopping, and scoping out the neighborhood where the pharmaceutical company was located. Michelle relaxed after the experience because the city was so large it was easy to feel unnoticed. The population of Guangzhou was similar to Los Angeles or New York City, but the population density was much higher as it was confined to a smaller amount of land. There were high-rises everywhere. Fortunately, there was an extensive public transit system so the air quality wasn't as bad as it was in Beijing or Shanghai. It also helped that the city was close to the coast.

At midday, they dined in a restaurant and enjoyed Cantonese food. After lunch, they took the subway system toward the headquarters of the pharmaceutical company. They also made a second journey into a more industrial area where the manufacturing occurred. From there they visited tourist destinations before returning to the apartment.

"So what are your thoughts for where I should drop listening devices tonight? Both locations of the pharmaceutical company?"

"I don't think so. The manufacturing area isn't going to be making espionage decisions. Those are coming out of their corporate headquarters. That's the only building we need to worry about. I wonder if we can find building plans anywhere for it? Let's save that question for the analysts."

Jason looked at his watch wondering about the time back in Virginia. The agency had analysts around the clock to handle questions like his. He reached out to the research division with this question and within an hour they had blueprints for the building in question. Rooms were marked in Chinese symbols, but the analyst had translated those symbols for the top floor of the building. Jason and Michelle thought that should be the target for listening devices. They picked offices and conference rooms, and Michelle could only hope they were empty when she planned to visit them. She couldn't imagine that security would have cameras inside of offices, so she should be safe.

They grabbed a nap and planned to visit the night markets on a food adventure. Jason was willing to try anything, while Michelle had taken anti-diarrhea medication and was very cautious about eating anything beyond her usual diet. She didn't need to be laid low by food poisoning. The tour went well and they returned to their apartment with happy tummies. They studied all the information around the operation again as they waited for the clock to tick down to one in the morning. Michelle could be efficient and take less than five seconds to plant the listening device in each location. Jason would silently worry at the apartment waiting for her return.

It went off without any complications and Michelle returned about twenty minutes after she left. "That went well. No one was around on that floor and the lights were turned down or off, but there's so much ambient light from the buildings around our target that I had no trouble seeing. Let's see if we can get some sleep and hopefully in the morning, we'll be on Chinese time."

Jason nodded and they went to sleep. The next morning, they read an email from Sheila and a summary from the analysts listening to the planted devices.

"More bad news out of San Francisco. It looks like an additional employee of the American pharmaceutical firm died just after the convention ended. The employee had planned to take extra days to tour the area and was found dead the next day by a housekeeping employee. This was a key scientist working on the breakthrough cancer treatment. Word from the company was they could go forward without the employee as they were far enough along, but they were distraught with her death."

"Her?" Michelle mused. "I hope it wasn't the bubbly woman I spoke with in the bar a couple of days ago. She seemed like such a nice individual and was so proud of the work the company was doing."

"Yeah, I agree with you. I thought the employees had security around them. I wonder how they got to her. Is there any new information about the first employee who died?"

"We know he died from a paralytic agent, but we don't know how it was administered. I don't see any new information from Sheila on that issue. I wonder if they used the same technique on both people?"

They resumed reading the information forwarded by the agency overnight and had their questions answered. It was in their water bottle in the hotel room.

"Are we sure that it's a Chinese firm behind these murders? I read the briefing the agency gave us on Chinese spies and that's not the way they do business. There have been two different murder weapons. They like to shoot or hang the enemy," Jason said. "Maybe we're in the wrong country?"

They heard a knock on the apartment door and they looked at each other and gathered up their belongings into their backpacks and put them on. Then they heard a second knock.

"Open up. Chinese police," At least that's what they thought they heard.

"Time to leave," Jason whispered. "Wait, can you go outside to the hallway and get their picture?"

"Okay," Michelle said as the knocking continued. She was out in the hallway and took pictures of what she saw, before going back inside to get them out of there. She had no more than wrapped her arms and legs around Jason, than the door burst open, but they were gone. She took them to her condo in Virginia, almost falling over when they arrived.

"That was close. What do you think that was about?" Michelle asked, her heart still pounding with the thought of confronting the Chinese police, or whatever agency they were with.

"Let's look at your pictures then call Sheila and let her know our plans have changed."

Michelle had captured men in uniforms with a man who might have been the building manager. None of the faces were clear enough so it was unlikely that the CIA could identify them.

"Do you think we left too soon?" Michelle asked.

"Look, you read the same agency briefing as I did on spies in China. They're not tolerated. They have a hundred-year history of executing anyone with the briefest of suspicions of working against the state. A lot of people were executed based on rumors. In the last century, they've had multiple civil wars, in addition to war with Japan and Taiwan. If we were handcuffed, you would have had to pull your disappearing act in front of witnesses. I think it was better to be safe than sorry. The agency needs to contact the person who arranged the apartment for us and see what happened with the police."

Michelle nodded and they put the call through to Sheila.

"So we're here in Virginia," Jason said.

"Why? Did you forget something?"

"No, we left in a hurry with our backpacks as the Chinese police were knocking on our door in an aggressive manner and the landlord was about to let them in. It would have been bad form for Michelle to do her disappearing act in front of them. She, on the other hand, felt a desperate need to get me out of there in a hurry. We sent you a picture of the gang in the hallway outside of our apartment."

There was silence on the other side of the call.

"Sheila?" Michelle asked.

"Yes, I'm looking at your photograph and thinking. I'm a little worried about our contact there. Just a moment."

There was hold music on Sheila's line and Jason and Michelle looked at each other.

"Okay, I've got our analysts running him down. I don't like that the police were knocking on your door."

"Yeah, well, we didn't like it either," Michelle mumbled.

"We've been discussing this case internally and wondering if we picked the correct country. We're suspicious about the ketamine agent that killed the two staff members of the biotech company."

"That's funny; we had arrived at that conclusion just as we

heard the knock on the door. So we didn't have time to pursue it," Jason said.

"We're doing some more research and we'll let you know. Until I have an answer for you, why don't you sit tight?"

The phone call ended shortly thereafter, and they looked at each other trying to decide what to do next.

"I hope she doesn't send us back to China. That history of executing spies really disturbed me. I almost wished I hadn't read that in the briefing documents as it put me on edge," Michelle said.

"You've been on dangerous assignments before, why is this one bothering you so much?" Jason asked.

Michelle weighed telling him the truth and finally said, "Because I have you to worry about. With my teleportation skill, short of being shot dead from behind, I can get out of any dangerous situation. However, with you, I've got to save you too. It's not easy wrapping myself around you when I'm under stress. What if I don't hold you as tight as possible and I leave, but you're still stuck somewhere with a bunch of murderers and torturers who want you to explain how I disappeared? The stakes are so much higher."

"Michelle, I told you, I'm a big boy. I've been with the agency a long time and in some tough situations and I've come home safely. I'll do so again. Maybe we need to change our cover and split up once we land in a country. First, we need to find out why the police wanted to search our apartment. Let's wait to hear back from Sheila. I love that you're worried about me, but that worry is making the two of us less effective for the agency."

"Have you been to another country like China before? Where they can and do spy on you?"

"Actually, I've been inside a Taliban camp and that was like staring death in the face. I couldn't wait to complete that assignment and get the hell out of there. I did get out of there alive and well. You forget I'm a great actor, while you feel uncomfortable acting. You have the superpower of teleportation and I have the superpower of acting my way out of tight spots."

"Okay. Do you think we should have stayed in the apartment?"

"No, as you would have given us away with nervousness. We made the right call. Now if the higher powers decide we're in the right country, we'll go back and figure out a new strategy. No one was hurt, including the agency by our disappearance. Besides, we planted listening devices in our room. Maybe Sheila's staff has some new information."

Michelle thought about his words for a while and nodded, "Okay, I'll get my act together after we hear from Sheila."

Jason decided to head to his home, thinking that he slept best there and whatever happened next was likely to include a lack of sleep. There was no news until halfway through the next day when they joined their boss on a video call.

CHAPTER 7

"It was all a false alarm. Our local contact is not allowed to sublet an apartment and you two were caught entering and leaving the apartment and appeared to be living there. The manager was quite confused as to how you got there, and he called the local police bureau for back-up to evict you. It was nothing more than a contract dispute. Our analysts are researching the issue to find out if this is the routine for all of Guangzhou or if we were just unlucky in our choice of accommodations," Sheila said.

"Any thought as to whether we were in the right country?" Jason asked.

"We don't have that question figured out yet. The U.S. has arrested economic spies connected to the Chinese government in the past, including someone who stole all the drug recipes from Gamma Drugs and then set up her own firm in China to make drugs. So, our mission is not a stretch of the imagination. I'll admit I'm stuck on the murder method—it's not the Chinese way. They generally like to lure someone to a location that they have control over or threaten family back home in China. If you're a

44

suspect inside China, then they send you to a labor camp or simply execute you."

"What countries other than China would you suspect?" Michelle asked.

"Any country that manufactures drugs, I guess. Germany, Switzerland, and the U.S. top the lists there. We're doing more research and should have answers later," Sheila said before she ended the call.

Michelle and Jason texted back and forth, then went their separate ways while waiting on the agency to make up its mind what to do next. The next day there was silence again. Michelle debated teleporting to a beach somewhere for a few hours, but then decided she needed to get more comfortable with China. With hindsight, and she thought given the infraction by the landlord they were facing, she thought that teleporting them out was the right thing to do. Maybe she needed to look at make-up or a disguise of some sort as a way to improve her acting skills. It would be a visual reminder to act. Something else to think about was staying in the U.S. and teleporting to China each day. If they decided on that later path, she would need to source a few safe teleporting landing spaces. A piece of their briefing documents discussed the cameras that are everywhere in China

Finally, Sheila set up a video call.

"We're going to have the two of you teleport each day. Of course, I can't explain your movement here, so if anyone asks, you're living in China. As that country is at nighttime when it is daytime here, you're gonna have some weird hours," Sheila said.

"Yes, but sleeping in my own bed and not worrying about waking up to the police arresting me means I'll be sharper with better sleep. I'm not a spring chicken anymore," Michelle said.

"Ditto," Jason said. "So what are we doing while we're in China? I assume we're going back to Guangzhou."

"Basically, the agency wants you to place additional listening devices in the two companies. They have obtained blueprints and have marked what they want. I'm faxing this over. There are some external locations which I assume Jason will take while Michelle handles the interior."

"That's it? That seems like a waste of our talents," Jason said.

"You won't say that if you get caught. Remember that you'll be on camera a good part of the time, and unlike the United States, you can't get away with an exaggerated homeless costume."

"True. I'll stop by and pick up whatever devices you want placed."

"Actually, I'll have Michelle teleport to my office as most of the agency thinks you two are in China. Take a look at the devices and locations and let me know if you need anything. It's coming up on sunrise in eastern China, so you'll be twiddling your thumbs for hours until you can go."

"Maybe I should do the exterior devices in the daytime. I'll wear a mask and walk with the flow of people; as I recall, the area around the pharmaceutical companies is fairly busy."

"That's a thought. Let me know what you and Michelle decide after you get the blueprints. I like to know where my case officers are located."

They ended the call, and an hour later, Michelle and Jason were studying the blueprints and discussing the street scene outside the pharmaceutical companies.

"I like your idea of day work as I think it's easier to hide, but I would be the first to admit that when I was planting devices the first time, I didn't look outside to see what kind of pedestrian traffic was on the sidewalk. Also, the parking lot below the building might be busy during the day and deserted at night. That would leave you vulnerable to any cameras watching the parking area," Michelle said.

"From a safety perspective, let's visit the area in the daytime and see where people and cameras are located, and then we'll go back just after midnight in China and evaluate the situation to see if we're better off doing what at which time of day."

"Okay, where should I teleport to? With cameras and people everywhere, I need somewhere safe."

"Good question. I'd ask Sheila for advice, but that's not a question she can put to the analysts. Are there any parks close to our target building? Maybe we could find some pictures of a park and guess a safe place to land."

A short time later they strolled through the park hand in hand like they were enjoying a relaxing leisurely time together. They knew they had about a five-block walk to the pharmaceutical house and so made their way in that direction. They carried their passports and had fancy cameras around their necks just to solidify their image as tourists.

As they were approaching the building, they discussed in low voices the pedestrian traffic and cameras they could see on the street. The parking garage was another problem. In the end, Michelle decided to do a teleportation trick where she moved across the floor at a breakneck speed from one corner to another. Jason was waiting for her nearby in a restaurant as she had gone to the toilet as her base to teleport beyond everyone's vision. He was stirring his coffee when he looked up and saw her return to their table.

"How's your stomach? Did something disagree with you? You were gone for a long time."

Michelle nodded and replied with a hand on her belly, "Yes, I needed to spend a little more time than usual in the toilet, but I feel fine now. Let's return to the park and from there head toward the river. I understand the views of the Pearl River are impressive."

They had no idea who was listening to them nearby, so this was all for show. They returned at a leisurely pace and found a quiet spot for Michelle to hug Jason and teleport them back to his condo. Milliseconds later they were safely back in Virginia. Michelle dropped a text to Sheila, letting her know of their return.

They returned to studying the blueprints and decided to place the exterior devices in the daytime and the interior and parking garage devices at night. The garage had seven levels, and yet the analysts only wanted listening devices on two of the levels near the elevators. They made changes to their appearance and Michelle returned them to the park with their pockets filled with listening devices which Jason proceeded to plant in the places requested. Michelle took them back to Virginia and again she changed her appearance and returned that night around midnight to finish placing devices in the requested locations.

She originally planned to take Jason with her, but he had no role in the planting of bugs in the interior and parking garage and it was faster for her to flit around by herself. In a short time, she returned to his condo, and they let their fearless leader know that the assignment was complete, and they were both safe on Virginia soil.

Michelle returned to her condo, and they waited for further instructions. Sheila arranged a video call and there was no new news out of China. The agency did receive some updated information from the San Francisco Medical Examiner. Both people who died had just the ketamine in their system; there were no other drugs.

"That's not a terrible way to go. You hallucinate, your heart races, then you're unconscious and you die," Sheila said. "If you're going to kill someone this way, at least knock them out before you do it to avoid the hallucinations. But on to new news. Our analysts have been listening intently to conversations in China and we're concluding that we are focused on the wrong country. I'm sending you to Basel, Switzerland, tomorrow."

"Okay. I like that as a better choice than China. At least they don't have as many cameras and people all around looking for CIA agents like Jason and me. Our lack of Asian features makes it obvious that we are foreigners in China."

"Yes. Basel is a pretty city and we're putting together a briefing for you. There are two companies that we're focused on. Basel is the heart of the chemical and pharmaceutical world, so it's no surprise that our killer might be coming from there. You're booked on a redeye flight to Switzerland leaving late tonight. I debated having you teleport and save the agency money, but there are times I like to play nice with other countries when my agents are working inside, and I feel that way about most of Europe. If their own spy agency notices your arrival, that's fine, but I don't think they will. I'll have materials delivered by four so you can pack the briefing in your suitcase. We have a new set of passports as well. I haven't looked up the weather—that will be your problem to plan for. Any questions?"

"Were there any people registered in the San Francisco hotel from whatever company in Basel we're targeting?" Jason asked.

"We're looking into that now, but keep in mind that company employees don't tend to be the murderers. I would think they would hire professionals; and given the lack of evidence left behind at the crime scene, I would say professionals were involved," Sheila said.

Michelle felt good about this change. While Sheila was talking, she did a little preliminary scouting of their new location. She didn't understand German any more than she understood the multitude of Chinese languages, but the second most spoken language was Italian, and she understood at least half of that language so she wouldn't be at such a complete loss for what was being said around her in this new destination. She also knew that Switzerland did not have cameras on every corner and police giving the suspicious eye to all strangers—especially those whose appearance lacked Chinese features.

CHAPTER 8

After studying their information packets, Michelle and Jason boarded the large commercial jet that would take them overnight to Switzerland. They were booked into a nice hotel on the river, had suitcases full of equipment, and knew the location of their target companies. Best of all, Michelle felt no threat from the average pedestrian on the street of the beautiful Swiss city.

"Let's drop our luggage off at the hotel as I'm sure it's too early to check in. Then we can head to a café and grab breakfast and maybe find our way toward the corporate headquarters of the companies that we're interested in," Jason said.

"That sounds like a plan. What a change in the weather—we went from sweltering subtropical southeastern China to a cool fall in Virginia and now to a city that expects snow in a month or two. I'll take Basel's climate any day."

After a taxi dropped them off at their hotel and they completed the paperwork for their stay, they followed the hotel's directions for charming places where they could find breakfast. They were quickly finding that many people spoke English among their multilingual talents.

They ordered their meals and took a moment to eavesdrop on the conversation around them. They heard mostly German, or what they thought German sounded like, and some Italian, but no other English conversations. This must be a restaurant that catered to few tourists. They spent some concentrated time listening to the Italian and then discussed what they heard.

"I think I heard the same as you. I really understood what they said except when they descended into a technical discussion. They were actually talking about drugs, but there are so many companies in this region, we don't know if it is relevant to our mission," Jason said.

"At least between English and Italian we can understand some of this region. Let's head over to the two companies of interest and scope out the landscape. Maybe we can find a variety of cafes and bars in the area, though after our experience in Venezuela, hoping to hear a random relevant conversation is a slow way to collect intelligence. I hope that HQ sends us the building floor plans so I can place some listening devices in time."

"Yes, we need to do that. We also need to explore the city like tourists as befitting our cover. So, let's take a look at the corporate buildings then head to a museum or some tourist site here. I'll check out the top tourist attractions. Then later this afternoon, we can return to the hotel and grab a nap. I know I'll feel like crashing, and if you have to place bugs in the middle of the night, your sleep will be disrupted too."

They spent time examining their target companies and the transportation alternatives in Basel. They headed to a nearby tram stop and made their way to a more industrial part of the city. After surveying the campuses of the two companies, they hopped back on a tram and headed toward a street market in a different part of the city. There, Michelle could relax and buy stuff like your average tourist. In this case, she got fruit and chocolate, and she tasted a variety of the famous Basel honey cakes from different bakers. They received word that Sheila wanted to meet with them in about two hours, which would be after they checked into their room. After eating food from the street vendors, they arrived back at their hotel and set up the encrypted technology for their call. On their end they had no new information for the agency.

"How's Basel?" Sheila asked.

"Much better than Guangzhou. Weather is cooler, food is understandable and edible, and we can eavesdrop on about half the conversations here," Michelle replied. "The hotel is old and beautiful and right on the Rhine River, so it's a gorgeous setting. It's also relaxing that I don't have to worry about the secret police getting hold of Jason or me."

"Such simple needs. On our end, we've put the company employees into protective custody. The National Institutes of Health had an empty lab, and we were able to move the company's work and its employees to a protected campus. We shouldn't have any more deaths, but we also aren't any closer to finding their killers. It is also hard to keep this operation a secret, which we need to do to keep the murderer guessing. There has been no evidence left behind in either of the deaths that pointed us one way or another."

"Did you learn anything from any of the listening devices I placed in Guangzhou?"

"Not yet. It's a painful process as we have a limited number of Chinese interpreters, and we had to place many devices and there're many conversations. I don't know if that will ever bear fruit. We want to focus on the two pharmaceutical companies in Basel as our technical experts say that they will take as great a financial hit as the Chinese company will and the impact may be greater. We've gotten floor plans for the companies. There are many buildings on each company's campus there in Basel. Our analysts have marked the blueprints of the buildings that they want you to plant devices in."

"Okay. I brought a bag of about one-hundred devices, and

we'll work on planting them tonight. How about any of the restaurants or pubs around the two campuses? Do you want to monitor conversations there?" Jason asked.

"We don't have unlimited resources to listen, and we have even fewer who can translate German," Sheila said.

"Don't you have some AI computer somewhere that could do that for you? Or at least screen conversations looking for words like *murder, death, cancer treatment, American company,* etc.? That seems like it would cut out a lot of conversations," Michelle asked.

"I haven't thought of that approach, and I don't know if we have the technology to do that. It sounds like we should, and I'll find out. Certainly, that would give us greater capacity to monitor locations across the world. We'll brainstorm on our end a list of phrases to look for beyond the ones you suggested. I have to say that on prior ops, we didn't have someone as skilled as you are at placing listening devices, so we haven't tried to listen on the large scale that we're doing with this case."

"Okay, we'll take a look at the blueprints to plan our work tonight. Can you think of anything else we should be doing?" Jason asked.

"We're researching the two companies in depth to see if they have any speaking engagements or if they're involved with any university labs. We'll want to get you inside either of those areas if they prove to be important. We've also done a complete search of the executives and their families and where they might be in the city in case we need to surveil them. I should have new information later today."

They wrapped up their call, and as they both felt the fog of traveling too many time zones, Michelle and Jason decided on a nap before looking at the blueprints to plan their night work. It was never good to plan the start of an operation with brain fog.

Two hours later and some sleep and a shower, they were refreshed and ready to plan the night.

Sheila's packet contained floor plans and interior shots of the pharmaceutical companies. Michelle needed those interior shots to be able to teleport inside to the right location. Michelle would have to do most of the work that night as almost all of the listening device locations were inside the buildings. It took her over two hours to complete the assignment, and fortunately she didn't run into anyone along the way. When they finished, they looked around for a late-night bar in the area around the two companies, but the two they visited were closing soon, so they headed back to their hotel to sleep.

CHAPTER 9

With nothing to do on behalf of the agency the next day, they discussed their next steps.

"Let's look up the photos of the leaders of these two companies. Maybe we can start following them to see if anything turns up," Michelle said.

"Are you hoping to see someone give someone else a briefcase of money to pay for assassination services?" Jason suggested.

"Stop making fun of my surveillance skills. We could be lucky, you know—in the right place at the right time."

"How did that work in Venezuela?"

"It didn't work, but you were in the right place to follow our billionaire industrialist's wife on our first case together. You were in the right place at the right time."

"That might be our only piece of luck for the year," Jason said smiling. He wasn't deliberately trying to irk Michelle, but she was such a novice at spying.

"Well, I'd rather be out doing something, so let's go. I've got the photos of the company leader on my phone."

She headed to the door and waited for Jason to follow. He

shrugged and decided to keep her company. She was right; they had nothing better to do.

After they exited the hotel and were mostly free of people who could eavesdrop, Jason said, "You know I had an assignment in Haiti some years back and the country was and is so chaotic that we surveilled people for a good month before we had useful information. That is the usual agency timeline."

"Well, if I have to spend a month in a foreign country, I'd rather do it in Switzerland than Haiti. If we're going to be here very long, we should start looking for new lodging. The place we're in must be expensive, and there are too many staff watching us coming and going."

"True. We'll discuss that on our next Sheila call. Let's park ourselves near one of the buildings and watch the flow of people and then we'll move on to the other company headquarters. Given my greater experience, we can discuss what we're seeing and hearing."

They searched for an area to sit and watch the flow of people near the first building. Jason made comments as people came and went.

"Where do people park? Are we missing a group of workers who drive to work?" Michelle asked.

"Good question. Let's stroll around the building and get an answer to your question."

They found a driveway down to a parking garage and decided to split up. Michelle would take the parking lot while Jason took the busy main door to the building. He was there for an hour when something got his attention. He looked around and texted Michelle.

Return to the front as fast as your legs will get you here.

That should give her the clue that Jason wanted her to walk to his position, not teleport there.

Michelle did a combination of jogging and fast walking and arrived at Jason's side quickly.

"What did you see?"

"One of the two men whose picture we looked at is right there," Jason said, nodding ahead to a man walking down the sidewalk nearly a block in front of them. They scrambled to keep up and hold hands as they were supposed to be lovers whenever they needed to actively surveil people. Another two blocks and the man entered a restaurant.

"Shall we have lunch?" Michelle asked.

"None of our suspects have seen us in person unless they were looking out of a building window at us. Let's dine and watch."

They entered a restaurant that looked out on the Rhine River. There were elegant white cloths covering the tables and beautiful glasses and place settings arranged on the few empty tables. In warmer weather, the view would be spectacular from the outdoor seating area. Today, with a temperature in the high fifties, their food would cool down too quickly. They noted their target and an empty table close by. Kudos to Jason for quickly spotting the man's location. To Michelle it looked like a sea of mostly men wearing boring dark suits. A waiter approached them, and Jason asked for the table near their target with the explanation that it was close to the terrace.

The waiter nodded and steered them to their preferred table and handed them menus. They both stared at the menu while concentrating on the conversation at the next table. Unfortunately, the voices were too soft and the ambient noise of the restaurant such that they couldn't hear anything.

As Michelle was closer, Jason asked, "Can you hear anything?"

"Not a word. I can't even tell what language they're speaking. This might be just a routine lunch."

"Unfortunately, you might be right. When lunch is done, you take the man that our suspect is meeting with and I'll follow the suspect. We can only hope that our food comes quickly, as does the bill. No dessert for us."

"As much as I'd love to try their desserts, I have to agree with your plan."

Jason leaned away from Michelle after adding, "Let's stick to a discussion about what we want to see here and maybe look at our Northern Lights pictures. That's a good cover."

Michelle nodded and launched into a discussion of the menu and Swiss cooking. Fortunately, her daughter, Ashley, was taking cooking lessons and in a recent phone call they had discussed various European styles of cooking. The meal continued uneventfully as did the conversation between the two men at the next table. They were lingering over their coffee, having paid their bill, when the two men appeared to wrap up.

"Let's go," Jason said. The two of them made their way out of the restaurant, in keeping with their role as tourists, and paused to photograph the buildings near the restaurant. In a short time, the two men exited the restaurant, shook hands, and departed in different directions. Jason and Michelle fist bumped and carried out their plan.

Michelle used her teleportation power to follow their suspect's dining companion. She would let him get nearly out of sight and then teleport to within twenty feet, causing surprised looks by nearby bystanders. Michelle merely smiled knowing that people would assume they were distracted and hadn't noticed that Michelle was there all along.

The man reached a carpark and Michelle looked around for a tall building that she could teleport to the top and then use to follow a car across the city. She found her building and was soon atop it, looking over the edge to follow the car. Basel was an old city and it made it harder to follow a car than, say, a grid city like Los Angeles. Still, she was able to keep up as car speeds were slower. In time, she could tell he was heading to the airport. They hadn't been able to get a picture of the man in the restaurant, so she planned to get one of him as well as his destination. She could avoid airport security by teleporting inside if she needed to, but hoped she would get the picture before then. The car followed the arrows for the rental car return. That told her he wasn't a local resident.

She followed him inside the rental office, but still his back was to her and she couldn't get a clear shot. She faded back into a group of people and followed him across the street to the airport. He checked in for first class to Singapore. Michelle took a chance and teleported into the last bathroom stall in the ladies' restroom. She arrived facing the toilet only to find a woman there.

Whoops. As quickly as she appeared, she moved on to outside the stalls next to the paper towel dispenser. Fortunately, the area was clear, and no one was looking at her. She quickly exited the bathroom before the woman in the stall left it to go to the sink and wash her hands. She went to the departure screen to find the Singapore gate and searched out her man. Finally, she was in a position to take a picture of him. She did so and sent it to Sheila so the agency could identify him. She then texted Jason with her whereabouts and checked in with him. While she had been tele-porting all over town, he had followed their man back to his office building and had been bored. He moved to a quiet alley, and she was at his side in no time.

"I think we've done all that we could with this person of interest at this time. Let's head over to the other pharmaceutical company and see if anything interesting is happening there," Jason said. "Besides, we planted cameras all over that building and that should allow the agency to gather lots of information."

"Yes. I don't know how long it will take the agency to identify the man in the picture I sent them and provide a dossier for us if he is interesting. By then, he'll be a world away in Singapore, or beyond. I can catch up to him when I need to in the future. I hope this surveillance thing doesn't go on for a long time. I'm not good at doing nothing for long periods of time."

"We're not doing nothing; we're watching our suspects."

"Okay, let me rephrase that: of all the skills and talents that I bring to the agency, watching people with a low probability of something happening is not my skill set. Nor is it my desired occupation. How do you have the patience for this?"

"We've watched people in the past on our missions. What's different about this?"

"We knew they were up to no good. For me this is like looking at endless police line-ups wondering who might be a criminal. In most cases, none of them are."

"Maybe this is spy school for you, and part of Sheila's grand plan," Jason said with a small smile.

Michelle grinned and said, "Right. I guess that's your way of telling me to suck it up and be happy with our comfy digs, good food, and working bathrooms. Things will get tense enough at some point. We'll likely be running for our lives, so I should enjoy the peace and quiet of the moment."

Jason gave her a fist bump as the two of them settled near the building housing the other giant pharmaceutical company. Despite several hours at the new location, they saw nothing and no one relevant to their case of the murdered lab company employees.

"Let's head back to the hotel and wait for new information and directions from the agency. We're wasting our time here," Jason said.

"Yes, it's disappointing. Let's walk back to our hotel as I feel like I've been sitting too much today."

Jason nodded and after a quick consultation with a map, they headed out for the two-mile walk back to their hotel. The weather was crisp, and the trees had lost about a quarter of their leaves. They both startled when they heard the crack of a branch behind them. In a practiced move, they each swung out to the side and turned around to see what was there. As they did, a man swinging his arm crashed forward nearly losing his balance. As he fought to regain his balance, they noticed what looked like an injector pen clutched in his hand.

CHAPTER 10

*J*ason and Michelle backed away from the man while trying to see everything they could about the man and his surroundings.

Did he have more than one injector?

Was he after Jason or Michelle or both?

How could they get a picture of him to identify him?

What was in the injector?

Was it the ketamine that was used in San Francisco to kill the lab employees?

Who is this guy?

Is he a professional and if so, what kind?

Is there anyone else around them who could help?

Likewise, they saw him also processing information trying to decide about what to do next. He had not expected Michelle and Jason to split up. They could see the wheels turning inside his head. Suddenly, he turned and took off.

"I'm going after him. I'm going to take that syringe from him and find out who he is," Michelle said, teleporting to a place in front of the man and then swinging her purse at him before he had time to react. He dropped to the ground holding his face.

Jason had taken off running behind their suspect and came upon him lying on the sidewalk. He quickly scanned the area and didn't see anyone there. He began searching the would-be assailant's pockets while Michelle snatched up the injector in a gloved hand and plopped it inside her purse. The man slugged Jason when he felt him rifling through his pockets.

Jason blocked the fist, and asked the man, "Who are you and who sent you to attack us?"

The man remained mute, so Jason repeated the question in Spanish and French and still no answer. The man was clearly attempting to sit up and make a run for it. Jason hadn't found anything in the man's pockets except his phone, which he took. He'd let the agency decode the device. They were in a foreign country and while they could call the police to report the attempted assault, they didn't want police attention. So, Jason shrugged and let the man go. They had his phone and his finger-prints on the injector; the agency would identify him. He looked Caucasian, but they had nothing more from an identity perspec-tive. Jason watched him disappear down the road.

"I don't think that was a random mugging attempt," Michelle said. "I just don't understand why he would come armed with only one injector syringe."

"I don't understand either, unless he made a mistake and that doesn't seem likely. When we split apart, I would have said he was aiming for you by the angle of his arm."

"Maybe he thought the female was the weaker target of the two of us. I wonder if we were seen from the windows at the pharmaceutical company. Maybe someone saw the two of us in San Francisco and now they're suspicious about what we're up to."

"Well, let's hustle back to the hotel and put a call in to our esteemed leader," Jason said, texting Sheila with an update and a request to chat in twenty minutes.

"Do you think the agency has forensic resources here? Otherwise, I could just deliver the injector to Sheila."

"I'm sure she'll ask you to bring it to her. You got a good picture of the man, right?"

"Let me look; he had a hand over his face a good part of the time he was on the ground," Michelle said, opening up the photo app on her phone.

They both looked at the pictures and none were a posed portrait, but one or two might do. Michelle sent those pictures on to Sheila. While they had other contacts in the agency, it was simpler and protocol to talk to their supervisor at Langley and let her coordinate the answers for the agents. They had been walking at a brisk pace and their hotel was in sight. Michelle could have teleported the two of them back to the hotel, but they both opted for the exercise.

Minutes later they were in their hotel suite waiting for the call from Sheila. In response to the photos, Sheila delayed their call to give her time to track down the assailant's identity. They sat down on a couch in their suite with a bottle of water and their laptop logged into the encrypted site and waited for Sheila to join them as they discussed their afternoon.

"So, you guys had an adventure today?" Sheila asked when she came on the call.

"Yes. I have an injector for the lab to identify and fingerprint," Michelle replied.

"My office is empty. Why don't you drop it off right now?"

"Okay."

Jason watched the freaky occurrence of Michelle at one moment being next to him on the sofa, then appearing on the screen in Sheila's office.

"I'm sorry, but can we take a minute to celebrate how freaking cool it is to see Michelle teleport four-thousand miles in the blink of the eye?"

Jason asked, and before he finished his sentence, Michelle had returned and was seated next to him on the sofa.

They looked at each other and smiled.

"It is pretty damn cool and don't tell anyone else, but you're my favorite agents just because I can worry less about you two getting out of danger. Okay, let's move on to this case. We identified the man at lunch today as the buying agent for an Australian pharmacy chain. You likely witnessed a standard business lunch."

"Bummer, I thought perhaps we might have a new clue," Michelle said.

"I'll schedule another call with you in a few hours once I have the results back on the injector or cellphone. They are likely the more interesting evidence. Why don't you run me through the scene?"

"Michelle and I were bored after all the surveillance today and decided to do a two-mile walk back to the hotel. I don't know that we were paying complete attention as to whether we were being followed. It's fall here so the ground is littered with twigs and leaves. We both seemed to recognize that a twig snapping close by was a bad sound. We sprang apart just as our man charged us from behind. His speed and force carried him straight through where we had been standing and we noticed a syringe in his hand. We all stared at each other for a moment, and he made the decision to run. Michelle teleported to an area in front of him and walloped him with her purse before he could defend himself, and I ran to meet the suspect. The man was on the ground, hands on his face, and I arrived to search his pockets. He tried to punch me, but by then I had patted down his pockets and had the phone. So, we let him up and he left on a run."

"Any injuries to you two?" Sheila asked.

"No."

"Any thoughts as to who the man was after?"

"We asked ourselves that question and I would say that he was aiming for me. However, whether that was because I was perceived to be a weaker partner, I don't know. We were the only people on that street, but it wasn't a bad area of town, so it didn't seem like a random act of violence.

"Hmmm. Okay."

Jason and Michelle could see the wheels of strategy churning in their boss's head and they waited for whatever question she came up with next.

"So where did someone see you and decide that you were a problem? We did identify him as someone into petty crime in Basel and it sounds like he's has upped his game by attacking you two."

"I don't know. We discussed that question and figured we either were spotted by someone inside the building, or maybe we got on someone's radar from San Francisco, or it was someone intent on robbing two stupid tourists."

"Do you truly believe the third option?"

"No," Jason said. "However, I can't imagine a low life criminal picking option three."

"Yes."

"So, Boss, what do you want us to do tomorrow? We're living it up in an expensive hotel with lots of eyes on us. We could move to a quieter rental. Do you want us to continue surveillance on the two companies?" Michelle asked cheerily.

"Why are you so cheerful?" Sheila asked, puzzled by her agent. Michelle was in her early fifties, but sometimes had the enthusiasm of a puppy dog.

"We didn't die, and we didn't even get hurt. We're living the high life in Switzerland, and we potentially brought the suspects out of hiding. Doesn't that make you cheerful?"

"Boss," Jason said. "They must have taught her that cheerfulness in spy school since she's the only one of the three of us who attended."

"Right."

"Man, I made one comment about spy school, and it's become the running joke between the two of you."

"Right. I'll call you back when I have new information. In the interim, our plan is for you to split up and conduct surveillance on the two pharmaceutical companies. Talk to you later."

The screen went dark, and Michelle and Jason looked at each other. "Some days, Sheila must have bad things happening among her agents as she seems short on her sense of humor," Michelle said.

"Maybe, or maybe her job is so serious that she can't laugh about most things."

"True, but how sad. Where do you want to go to dinner?"

"Let's just walk down the street until we find something. Let me shower and change clothes and you should change clothes as well."

"Why?"

"If anyone follows us from this hotel, it makes it harder to spot us as compared to what we were wearing earlier. That's a spy school 101 technique."

"Oh. That makes sense. See you in a few," Michelle said, heading into her bathroom with a smile on her face.

A short time later they set out from their hotel to a restaurant recommended by their concierge. After the fancy lunch, they wanted something more relaxed for dinner and were heading to a sports pub that was a four-block walk away. They used the selfie screen on their phones to check out who was behind them when they couldn't see reflections in store windows. So far they noticed no one following them. They reached the pub with no adventures along the way. After ordering beer and their main courses, they watched the crowd of people. They were, for the most part, watching soccer games.

"I don't follow European soccer. It's hard enough to follow the major sports in the U.S. How about you, Jason?"

"No. I'm in the same boat as you. I'll occasionally watch a soccer match at home, but all the running back and forth doesn't float my boat. I couldn't even tell you which club is the best."

"Hey, at least you know, they are called 'clubs'; that's not a term we use at home. When you say the word 'club,' it makes me think of a place you pay for membership. Did you notice the woman seated at the bar?" Michelle asked.

"Yes. I'm impressed you noticed her."

"How could I not? She glanced over at us about five times, and she seemed uncomfortable sitting at the bar by herself. I wonder what she is up to?"

"Let's sit here awhile and watch. I didn't see her on the street on our way here. I'm pretty sure she arrived after we did. But if she didn't follow us, how did she know we would be here?"

"Good question. Maybe we should look through our stuff just to make sure we aren't giving off signals. That would be ironic if while we were out placing listening devices, someone was in our hotel room placing GPS devices," Michelle said.

They watched her until the pub began to empty out as the soccer game was over. She consumed multiple glasses of water and a meal at the bar. Jason was under the impression she wasn't a local and she had no interest in the game on TV as she never demonstrated any emotion for the success or failure of either team.

"I doubt she has a weapon on her as that requires a permit in this country. That's not to say that she abides by the rules; rather that the public frowns upon such behavior and would call her out for doing so," Jason said.

"We could go on offense and walk up to her and ask her politely why she's staring at us," Michelle suggested. "It's a public space, so I can't see her doing anything violent here. I'll go up to her now and ask what she thought of her food. Did you see what she ate for dinner?"

"She ate fish and chips."

"Perfect I'll have no problem striking up a conversation on that target. If you see me pitch to the floor, run! That means she has an injector gun."

"I'm not going to run. I'm going to call 112, which is the emergency number here, as you will likely need respiratory support until the drug wears off or it can be countered. Remember the lab employees in San Francisco?"

"Good point. Wish me luck," Michelle said, reaching a fist bump toward Jason. They touched and she was off to the bar.

"Hello," Michelle said to the woman who had been giving them looks all evening.

Michelle had picked a time when the woman's attention was not focused on her and Jason and so she startled the woman by her appearance and question. Still, the woman recovered fast and shook her head as though to convey that she didn't speak English. So Michelle honored the woman with greetings in French, German, and Spanish. Still the woman didn't smile. The bartender dropped off a drink and said to her in English, "Here's your soda with a touch of lime."

"Ah, you do speak English. Did you like your fish and chips?"

"Why do you want to know? You already ate your dinner."

"Yes I did. I had the same dish as you and wondered if you enjoyed it as much as I did."

"None of your business."

The way the woman responded told Michelle lots of things about her. First, she spoke English with a European accent. Second, she was rude to Michelle and people were simply not rude in Switzerland. Michelle would bet twenty dollars that the woman was spying on her and Jason. She debated what question to ask next and decided on the truth.

"Why have you been staring at my husband and me all night?"

Michelle could see that the woman was debating what to say in response to her question. She had caught the woman off guard by approaching her and asking her the obvious question.

She saw the answer in her face; she was going to brave it out and lie.

Michelle sighed, waiting for the lie to come her way.

"I don't know what you're talking about. I haven't been staring at you all night. That's the trouble with you Americans—you think the world revolves around you."

Two could play at this game, Michelle decided.

"So you were surprised that I had the nerve to approach you at the bar, and then you decided to try and lie your way out of my question. That tells me everything I need to know. Goodbye."

She walked back to where Jason was casually awaiting her return. He elevated an eyebrow in question.

"She decided to lie her way out of my questions and said we Americans were self-centered and thought the world revolved around us and that she hadn't been staring at us all night. I told her I recognized a lie when I saw one and I left. She's not as good at disassembling as you are, Jason. Did you get a picture of her?"

"I did get a nice picture of her mostly because she glared daggers at you when you left to return to our table."

"So what do you think our next steps are?"

"Walk back to our hotel keeping an eagle eye out for any muggers and looking around for her to follow us, but I don't think she will."

"Why not?"

"Because she doesn't have to. While you were chit chatting with her, she dropped something into your right pocket."

"It's a good thing that you're watching out for me."

"I've always got your six, partner."

"What does that mean?" Michelle asked. "I would hear it once in a while on the job in California, but I never asked what it meant."

"Six refers to six o'clock, which is behind you. It was used in WWII and pilots would say 'I've got your six,' meaning they were watching the rear of the plane against attacks."

Michelle nodded at his explanation and reached into her pocket and at first didn't feel anything, then her fingers made contact with what felt like a crumb and she pulled it out to look at it as they were exiting the bar.

"Wow, this is good technology. It's so small. What should I do with it?"

"Let's keep it with us for now and we'll drop it in the pocket of someone checking out tomorrow in the lobby," Jason said.

"Okay. Do you think it is a listening device as well as GPS?"

"No. It's too small." Jason said. He took out his phone and hit a few buttons. Michelle realized he was using the selfie function to scan the street behind them.

"Anyone back there?" Michelle asked, while she fake posed for a picture.

"Perhaps, but our hotel is just there so I don't think there is any trouble that can be started at the moment. Maybe we're just under surveillance."

"How do you think we came to be followed?"

"I don't know. Let's talk about it when we get back to the room."

"Are you sure that's not a listening device?"

"Well if it is, they've heard our entire conversation," Jason said and then gave Michelle a look that said, "don't talk anymore." They entered the hotel and reached their room without incident. Michelle watched as Jason put the device in a baggy and then put the baggy in a glass of water in the bathroom. He then pulled a scanner out of his luggage and slowly scanned the entire room. They found several more devices.

They wrote notes back and forth to each other trying to decide what to do. In the end, they used the old spymaster trick of turning on the TV in the room and moving into the bathroom after they removed the devices from there including the one in the glass of water and turning on the ventilation fan.

"This is bad news for us. I don't know how much they heard

over the past couple of days. I hope they didn't hear you tell me about the teleportation conversation with your kids. We don't want that cat out of the bag. I think we should go home to Virginia now so we can chat and then come back to the room just to sleep. We'll also want to find new digs in the morning."

CHAPTER 11

$\mathcal{M}$ichelle moved the two of them to Virginia and then they called Sheila to let her know what they were doing.

"That's interesting," was Sheila's first response. There was silence over the line as she thought about what had happened and what their response had been.

"Did you bring any of the devices home with you?" Sheila asked.

"I was afraid to do that. We didn't know if they were GPS, or listening, or both. Jason has never seen them before, nor have I. I could head back to the hotel and overnight them to Langley."

"Yes, why don't you do that? We'll find a new home for you tomorrow as there seems to be random activity in Basel that may or may not be related to the case. Regardless, someone is trying to spy on or track two CIA agents. We need to know why and how they identified you two as worthy of spying."

"We've been trying to answer that question ourselves. The only thing we could come up with was we were caught by someone inside one of the drug company buildings as we were placing the surveillance devices and that someone wanted to know more about us. I suppose they need to worry about industrial espionage."

"That's true. It would be ironic if you were caught up in their surveillance of industrial spies. Instead, they started following real spies and must wonder what they stumbled into. I wish I knew how long they were listening. If it is from the drug company windows, then at most it's been twenty-four hours, right?"

"I think less than that. They would have followed us back to the hotel at some point and then needed us to leave before they could plant anything. That would have been this morning," Jason said.

"Do you have any further information on the phone, the picture, or the injector?" Michelle asked.

"Just because you can span the globe in milliseconds doesn't mean our lab can likewise pull off such magic. I have no report yet or identification of the woman in the photo."

"Okay. Well, I guess I'll get a good night's sleep after I get one of those tracking devices taken care of for you. Jason and I will head back in the morning to check out and move to a new location. Maybe we will head to the airport, and then take transit back to our new digs so whoever is trying to track us fails."

"Okay," Sheila said, ending the call.

Michelle and Jason looked at each other and shrugged, then Michelle added, "Why don't I meet you at your condo early in the morning tomorrow so we can head back to Switzerland?"

"Okay, but text me once you return from Basel. I want to know that you didn't run into any problems in our hotel room."

"Will do. Where will I find an overnight mailer to use in Basel?"

"Why don't you visit the office of one of the major U.S. shippers and tell them you're heading there and will want to overnight something small that fits into an envelope back here and see if they will let you prepay and make a label. Otherwise, I would bring the device in the baggy inside something that blocks satellite signals like a lead box or faraday box."

"I have a series of those Russian dolls that fit inside of each other. I could put it inside one of those with lots of foil around each doll . . . that should confuse the signal."

Jason smiled at her idea. "There's a novel use of Russian dolls. Good luck."

Michelle did as Jason suggested and visited a shipping company for a prepaid envelope. Fortunately, they were familiar with her type of request and she didn't have to resort to taking her Russian dolls and a box of aluminum foil with her to their hotel room in Basel. She teleported to the hotel room, making sure it was empty. Who knew who might have the nerve to go into their hotel room with them not there?

The room was empty and Michelle quickly gathered up three devices, put them in the envelope, and took them down to the lobby desk and asked them to have the envelope be picked up by the shipping service in the morning. They informed her of a box she could drop it off in that was just down the street. Michelle thanked them for that piece of information and sought out the shipping box. It would be emptied in the early morning, which was good news for the device to reach the United States sooner. She then teleported back to Virginia, texted Sheila and Jason with the results of her night's work, and tried to get some sleep before meeting Jason early in the morning.

She met Jason the next morning and teleported them into their room in Basel. They checked out, taking a taxi to the airport, then took a bus from the airport that deposited them close to their new location according to the information that Sheila had given them. It was an apartment rental closer to the pharmaceutical companies, yet they were still within walking distance of the river where so much activity took place around the city. As well as they could tell, they were not tracked, especially as they scanned their luggage and removed the trackers from it and managed to drop the devices into the luggage of someone else at the airport.

They settled into the two-bedroom apartment, happy to be anonymous in their lodging. A trip to a local grocery store supplied them with the bare necessities. They had another call with Sheila that afternoon and they sure hoped she had some new information.

"Have you settled into your new apartment?"

"Yes, it's nice and we'll be able to live quiet lives here," Jason said.

"Well, we identified the man who came after you with the injector, which was filled with potassium by the way. He's a low-level criminal known to Swiss authorities. We'll leave him be as we don't want to alert Swiss authorities to your presence."

"What's the deal with potassium?" Jason asked.

"It was enough of a concentration to *screw up the electrical conductivity of the heart and kill you,* it says here on the piece of paper the lab sent me."

"Yikes," Michelle said. "It seems so bucolic here, I forget they have assassins."

"So, someone knows we're looking into the deaths of the lab folks in San Francisco. Have they followed us to Switzerland, or did we end up on their radar for some other reason?" Jason asked.

"The only thing that makes sense to me is that you have been recognized by someone who was there in San Francisco. You haven't been in Basel long enough to look so suspicious that someone is out hiring an assassin," Sheila said.

"Would you send us pictures of everyone who was at the conference? I'd love to walk around with a camera on my head scanning for a facial match of anyone in one of those pictures."

"Yeah, well don't get your hopes up as we don't have any walking satellite head cameras yet. Have you been watching fantasy TV recently, Michelle?"

"Ouch. I guess we don't have a Q who works for the agency designing cool stuff."

"Your ability to teleport is cooler than anything that James Bond's Q designed for him, and we're getting off-track here. I don't have the results on the woman from your pub yet, but I expect to have it in another few hours. We don't have unlimited resources here and we had a rush job going on another project."

"Okay. We'll lay low until we have a read on how we might have been identified," Jason said.

The video ended shortly after that, and Michelle and Jason looked at each other.

"She must be stressed by another assignment at the agency. I guess there's nothing for us to do until we get new information. I'd say we should continue surveillance on the drug companies, but if we have been spotted by someone at one of the companies, it would be easy to avoid us."

"If we do any more surveillance, we'll need you to fetch some disguises from home. We can't put our bare faces in that area of town again," Jason said.

"Yes. Are you good at memorizing faces? There were hundreds of people at that conference, and I don't know how I'll remember any of them looking at pictures."

"I think it will be pure luck if we recognize someone here in Basel from their professional photo in San Francisco. We should toast ourselves, by the way, for avoiding the potassium syringe. That would have been a painful and sure death."

"Yes, I must agree with you on that. It seems so peaceful and calm surrounded by these beautiful mountains, but there are killers lurking ready to end our lives. If that man had got you, Jason, I could have teleported you inside the ER at Johns Hopkins, but we wouldn't know what your problem was. Maybe I'll look up the remedy or reversal agent since that's the bullet we're dealing with."

Michelle researched potassium and put together a plan on

what to do if confronted with that agent including a picture on their phones of the drug therapy they would need to survive the potassium attack.

They lazed around the apartment brainstorming how they could have been identified. In the end, Michelle fetched disguises from Virginia. Jason had stuff in a closet at home that he used for various assignments and Michelle headed to a Halloween store to buy a few essential supplies. In no time they were dressed and out the door searching for new clues in Basel.

Sheila sent a text identifying the woman and it was surprising. She worked for one of the two companies that they had under surveillance. In fact, she was related to the founding family— a cousin or something. It was the company that they had tried to spy upon at lunch.

"So we were either tagged while we were in that restaurant or before when we were doing surveillance on the building," Michelle said to Jason as they strolled down the street.

"I think it was likely outside the building. Who knows if they had security cameras focused on where we were standing? Let's see if we can find a popular coffee bar that we can hang out in yet be able to see our target building."

They found a perfect location and were able to watch the activity around the company. They took turns facing each other and staring out the window. Still, by the end of the day, they had no new information.

They were walking back to their apartment discussing the lack of new leads and the hard wooden chairs they had sat on in the coffee bar.

"Let's not do that again. Maybe we should head home and then come back when there's something to do," Michelle said.

"You need to learn patience. You know we're in the right place as we nearly got injected with an agent that would have killed us quickly if left untreated. That's a good sign. Someone has us on their radar."

"Yes, but we moved away, so they don't know where we are yet to try and cause trouble. Maybe we shouldn't go in disguise—make it easy for them to find us."

"True," Jason said, thinking about it. "We moved out of the fancy hotel to have more privacy, save money for the agency, and be closer to our suspects. I see no conflict in letting them know where our new lodging is despite the fact we tried to hide that by going to the airport in a taxi and riding the bus here to our new digs."

"We need some extra security on our door, though. I don't want to wake up with someone standing over me with a potassium syringe. From what I read about that, we'd have just a few minutes to get help from a hospital, and it would be an awful experience."

"Agree. I have some stuff at my apartment for us. Take me there and we'll pick it up and set it up here. I have battery-operated motion detectors and extra locks we can put on the windows without damaging them. We should add a camera in the lobby."

"That's a thought. We'll have to set up a laptop to record. We could ask the agency to do it, but it's something we can handle ourselves and it's not like we're overworked at the moment. Do you have the type of cameras that only record motion?"

"I don't think so, but electronics stores are still open, so give me a list of what you want and I'll get the stuff." They knew they could get stuff from the agency, but it was faster sometimes to just buy it and bill the agency.

In under an hour, Michelle was back with a backpack of purchases and double-sided tape. They had their cameras installed, then began to cook dinner. Their phones had an app that signaled every time something activated the motion detector. Their apartment building was five stories high with two apartments on each floor. Hopefully the smallness of the building meant that the camera would not be triggered too often.

They got their first alert and watched as someone walked in

and checked the mailbox before disappearing. Yes, that was a resident. They turned off the alerts after they became annoying, promising themselves they would look at the recording later and set off for a local pub to people watch. It was evening and they thought they needed to show their presence to the pharmaceutical company in daylight. Maybe the woman would find them, but they doubted it. After a few hours and some great pub food, they returned to their new home-away-from-home to sleep.

At breakfast they discussed their plan for the day. They would be together and apart surveilling the buildings. They had earpiece communication so they could chat when they wanted to, and the goal was to attract the attention of someone. In the afternoon, they would return to the apartment for the encrypted conversation with Sheila. They had an uneventful walk home and didn't notice anyone following them. The next day was forecasted for rain, so they would be unable to use the same tactic two days in a row.

Sheila had some changes when she called that afternoon.

"I'm going to separate you two for a few days as I need Michelle's help with another agency issue. We have an agent who made contact with someone high in the Russian military hierarchy and we need to get him out of a tight situation. I'm worried that he may have been detained by the SVR, which is the agency name for their secret police. I need you in my office in about ten minutes to go over your role there. Any new developments on your end? Once I get my other agent safe, I'll strategize with you two on the next steps."

"Nothing new to report, Sheila," Jason said. "We're trying to get noticed by someone who means us harm, but we're failing to do that. Tomorrow, rain is forecasted and so our current strategy won't work in that weather. I'll just be around the city tomorrow until Michelle returns."

"Okay, see you in a few minutes, Michelle."

"Geez, there's nothing going on here, so you get to have all the excitement elsewhere."

"Yeah. Well, if you get into trouble, just call and no matter where I am in the world, I should be able to reach you and get you out of danger."

"That's a nice offer, but I doubt anything the least bit dangerous will happen in your absence."

"Yes, hopefully, those aren't 'famous last words.' See you," Michelle said, and she was gone.

CHAPTER 12

Michelle appeared in Sheila's office on time.

"What do you need my help with?"

"We've been using an agent to keep us informed about Russian troop movements. We haven't heard from him in about four hours. He's in a high-risk job so we have hourly check-ins."

"Where is he located? Moscow? Has he ever failed to contact you before?"

"Yes, Moscow, and this is his first failure. I want you to go to Moscow and search his apartment and the other places we know him to be using on this assignment. We have another agent there who has been searching for him, but he hasn't made any progress in the past four hours. I can't lose this agent."

"Okay. I need pictures of the missing agent, your other agent, and the places he haunts in Moscow."

Sheila had that ready to go, explaining each one.

"I'm going to go home to change my clothing as I'm not dressed for Moscow at the moment. Do you have a new phone for me?" Michelle asked, knowing that Sheila usually handed out phones for new assignments. Each phone was specially encrypted for the country they were heading to.

"Yes, here you go. I need you to go as soon as possible."

"I'll just change clothes and be in his apartment in about ten minutes. I'll text you when I'm there."

"Thank you and good luck."

Michelle disappeared before her eyes and Sheila shook her head at the wonder of it all. Twelve minutes later she had a text from Michelle that she was in Eric Karros's apartment. When she teleported, she landed in the shower as Sheila had provided photos of all the interior rooms and figured that the shower was the least likely place to have a camera watching the interior of the agent's apartment. She found no technology in the apartment. No phone, no laptop, no plugs even for technology. She searched for his backpack and then began looking in unusual places—toilet lids, air vents, carpet edges—for anything hidden and she found nothing. She also looked for cameras that might have been used to spy on Eric. She also did a scan for devices and found a few in the apartment. The agency identified them as Russian devices, so they were not placed there by Eric to watch his own digs.

Michelle debated whether to walk out of the apartment or teleport somewhere else in Moscow. She didn't want to be caught on camera disappearing, but if someone already observed her on camera, then she'd best get a move on. She opened the drapes and looked out at a dreary Moscow in the late afternoon. It was an hour ahead of Basel, so at least she didn't have time-zone confusion. She looked around for a place to teleport to and didn't see anyplace safe and without people. She supposed that people were on their way home from work. So, she opted for her back-up solution to this kind of dilemma—when you couldn't go low, you went high—and so she teleported to a nearby building roof where she hoped to find a ground-level destination where she could go next.

It was in the high forties temperature-wise and dropping, which gave her an excuse to have a hat and parka on and keep her head down to avoid any cameras that might be on the street. She saw her next location at street level and was soon walking along the street. Where should she go next to find the missing agent? It was a huge city, and wandering around wasn't likely to help. She texted Sheila's other contact and set up a meeting location. He suggested a café on the other side of the city according to the map app on her phone. No problem. She would teleport to a nearby tall building, then find a ground-level location to go to once she saw that the coast was clear. Minutes later found her walking into the café to meet Michael Miller, the other agent on the lookout for Eric. The café was noisy and busy and was clearly transitioning into happy hour judging by the drinks in people's hands. In keeping with tradition, she had Michael order her a beer. He spoke Russian and she did not and she didn't want to navigate a conversation with a food service worker in Russian.

"I searched his apartment. There was no technology, but there were a few cameras planted. Unfortunately, I don't know if those were there all along or were placed there after he went missing. Given that he's been missing about five hours, I'm thinking the cameras were there before."

"I would agree with that assessment. It's standard procedure to search for devices every time you enter your abode here in Russia and depending on what kind of devices you find, you organize your life around them. If they're listening devices, you change where you have important conversations. If there are cameras, you just remember where they are and try to do nothing to raise the attention of anyone on the other end of the lens."

"Aren't you worried that you're about to be detained when you see those devices?" Michelle asked.

"No, because some of the devices don't work, and some are decades-old technology. You try not to take it personally. For cameras, I'll try to darken the room in broad daylight, then I'll place tape over the lens and go about my business. Listening devices are easy to run away from."

"Did you know Eric's schedule?"

"I did. We generally shared our schedules every day so if either of us went missing, there would be an effort to trace our actions. Eric had a meeting today with a high-ranking Russian military officer who supposedly wanted to give away some of his army's plans for Ukraine. The meeting was supposed to take place across the street just past the kiosks for the metro station," Michael said, moving his eyes to a building across the street with a constant flow of people.

"So, we need to hack into cameras in that subway station to see what his movements were, assuming he reached the meeting location. I wonder if this official just wanted to take him into custody as a traitor to the motherland?"

"That sounds simplistic, but go ahead and send the agency nerds the idea of hacking into the cameras."

"Aren't you a cynic?" Michelle said. "Do you have any better ideas? Moscow is a big city; he could be hiding on his own in many locations, or if he has been taken by the SVR, there are many cells for political prisoners, right?"

Michael sighed, "Sorry. You're new here. Moscow will make you paranoid in no time. You can't relax your guard. I'm deeply worried that he may be in detention, and it will be next to impossible to get him out."

"Hey, last week I was in Guangdong so trust me when I say I understand your paranoia. We just need to find him."

"I thought you came from Basel?"

"I did, but just before Basel, I was in China. At least in Russia, people can't tell you are a foreigner by looking at your face. There was no hiding that I was a Caucasian foreigner in China. Let's find where Eric is located and we'll work to get him out of there. I don't speak Russian, just Spanish, so I haven't a clue about conversations going on around me."

"Why did Sheila send you here? I know the agency has other, Russian-specific agents."

"I have a special skill that may come in handy depending on

where Eric is located. I'm the best in the world with my skill. Let's hope I don't have to use it and Eric is hiding for some reason."

"What's your skill?"

"It's classified. I can't share that with you."

Michael looked at her, puzzled, and then shrugged and said, "Tell Sheila to do camera research for us then."

Michelle took a moment to send a text to Sheila for the analysts to handle.

"Do you have a place to stay tonight?" Michael asked.

"I do."

I'll be safe in my bed in Virginia, she thought, not worried about Russians breaking into a hotel room.

Sheila responded that the analysts were working on it. She looked over at the station and said, "Let's go look and see what is inside the station. I can't imagine there will be a clue there, but who knows?"

Michael nodded as he didn't have a better suggestion.

Michelle had never been to Russia and certainly had never seen their subway system, and she had to admit she was impressed. The station they were at was immense with beautiful marble, a bright yellow ceiling, and gold-plated motifs.

"Wow, this is beautiful, and there's no graffiti to screw it up. I suppose that's because of all the cameras and stiff penalties for defacing public property."

"Yeah, pretty much."

They looked around and then turned and left as they were wasting their time and risked getting caught on the ubiquitous security cameras.

"Where else have you looked for him?" Michelle asked.

"He favored a café for coffee and a bookstore. I checked both of those locations."

"Do you have any idea where he would be taken if he was captured? Do you know where political prisoners go in Moscow?"

"There's an old prison in the middle of Moscow that is the

usual first stop for political prisoners. Are you planning on breaking in there to search for Eric?" Michael asked with a smirk.

She felt like saying, *as a matter of fact, yes.*

Instead, she said, "So if he was picked up inside the station, he would have been moved in some kind of transport vehicle to the jail. That is if he made it to this meeting. Do you guys keep an eye on each other when you set up meetings that could turn out badly?"

"Yes, we do that sometimes, but Eric didn't ask for my help on this one. We back each other up perhaps about a third of the time. Mostly, we do that in hope that someone knows where the other goes if we get captured by the SVR."

"Do you have hidey holes around the city?"

"That's standard procedure when operating in this country. Each of us has a couple of places we've sourced as hiding spots when times get tough."

"Can you share them with me, or have you looked in them?"

"Each of us has our own spaces that we don't share with other agents as we don't want someone else to reveal them under interrogation."

"Makes sense," Michelle said, gulping at the thought of Russian interrogation. She remembered the captain she had rescued from a cold prison in eastern Russia. That cell and prison were awful. She visited him a few nights before the night she broke him out of prison. Specifically, she gave him nutrition to make sure he had the energy to run. She hadn't seen what the man had gone through prior to reaching that cell, and it was before she learned she could have simply wrapped herself around the man and teleported him back to the United States.

"Okay. I'd like to search hidey holes on my own. It's likely less suspicious if we break up. Where typically do you find them?"

"Usually in subway stations—there are all kinds of hiding spaces. I'll also look for abandoned buildings in the city I'm in. I rarely pay rent in a second location."

"Okay, I'll start by searching this station. See you later," Michelle said walking away.

She knew it was kind of rude on her part, but she had a sense of urgency from Sheila and she thought she likely had all the relevant information from Michael. Besides, she wanted to do some fast moving around Moscow, but not in front of anybody or any camera. She liked the idea of searching the train tracks, but she would have to be careful not to get killed by a train. Her ability to get out of the way in the blink of an eye was critical to this search.

She walked around searching for the location of the train tracks. She planned to go look down a tunnel of any track where the train was in the station. That was the time people were not likely to pay attention to her and if the train was in the station, then the track behind should be empty.

She traveled down the first track and decided she needed some night-vision glasses and returned home for those. It was hard to see in the dark, and she could imagine herself not seeing someone already down the track and getting slugged in the back of the head and dying down there when a train roared over her. Yuck.

She had located an alcove before her departure, so she could come back to it with goggles in hand without being killed by an incoming train. She was back inside the train tunnel in no time, and she could see much better. It was creepy. She could see shapes moving, both human and animal.

She pulled up the picture of Eric Karros in her head and searched for him among the faces down in this area. It wasn't easy to do as people were hunched and often wearing hoods. If someone was the right build and might be the agent, she got closer and whispered, "Eric?"

She hoped it didn't mean something bad in the Russian language but given the blank look she'd gotten the first time she uttered it, she doubted it. One thing was clear, there were few women down here. She hadn't spotted one yet and so that made her stand out. She made another quick trip home to disguise her gender. She bulked up her middle hiding her bosom and hips and changed hats to ensure her hair was tucked up. On the other hand, teleporting in the dark had never been easier.

She heard a rumbling in the distance and thought that likely meant a train was on its way into the station. She looked around for a place to stand out of the way, found it, and stood there as the rumbling got closer and she saw lights. She pushed the googles up onto her forehead and leaned into her space as the train roared by with screeching sounds of brakes as it approached the station. Michelle realized she should've done a search of how frequently the trains arrived before she came down here. She looked around her and no one was close by, so she went home for the third time to find the frequency of trains so she could set an alarm to look for safe spaces between her searches of the tracks.

Moments later she was back and again sizing up people who would fit her description of Eric. There seemed to be a human about every hundred feet underground. She supposed it was a way to stay away from the police and to stay warm. The temperature wasn't hot, but given how far below the surface the train tracks were located, she would bet that the temperature was consistent. With the cold and brutal winters in Russia, these tracks were likely a good place to live. Perhaps the trains didn't run at night. As she moved further down the tracks, she thought she was probably looking for a needle in a haystack. If someone didn't want to be discovered down here, they wouldn't be. Furthermore, this was just one track. There were two different lines that came to the station, so she should search the area in front of the station as well as behind it. It was time to consult with Sheila as to a better strategy.

CHAPTER 13

*M*ichelle teleported back to her apartment and texted Sheila to see if she was available.

Yes.

Michelle was standing in her boss's office a moment later. She was still wearing the parka and had the night-vision goggles pushed up on her forehead. She took off the parka and padding as she quickly became overheated.

"I was searching the train tracks at the station where Eric was supposed to meet the military leader. There are a fair number of humans who live in that subway system. There was one about every hundred feet. There are two train lines that meet at that station. The train tracks are an excellent place to hide. It is dark and there are many spaces to lean into so you don't get run over by a train. I understand that the subway lines in Moscow are one of the biggest in the world, and I can search in the dark for days and not find Eric. I need a new strategy. Do you have any suggestions?"

"The next place to search would be prisons in Moscow."

"Here's the problem with that suggestion—they like to pack

several people into one cell. I can't see myself teleporting from cell to cell without alerting the world as to my special skill. Have your analysts hacked into the security cameras at the station to see if they can locate Eric?"

"They are working on it, but there are problems. It's a large system and each station has many cameras. I understand our analysts have been able to hack into the system and maybe in an hour will be able to look at the camera footage."

"Since I was physically in the station, I might be of some help to the analysts. Where are they located? I'll go join them."

"I think I'll join you," Sheila said. "I don't have any better ideas on where to find this agent. Follow me."

The two women spent the next hour looking at computer screens in their search for Eric Karros. Finally, they spotted him and then it took time to follow him on the cameras. He looked at his watch and then left the area where he was supposed to meet the military leader. A short time later they spotted him on a new camera wearing a different hat and jacket. Apparently, something had spooked Eric and he changed his plans inside the station. They followed him to one other location and then lost him.

"I guess the good news is he hasn't been recorded on camera as being detained by Russian authorities. The next question is, where did he go and how do we rescue him?"

"Let's go back to my office," Sheila said, after instructing the analysts to contact her if they discovered any other images in the future.

As soon as Sheila closed the door, Michelle said, "I guess I'll head back to the station and the train tracks. Any other suggestions on where to look?"

"No. We don't have a tracker on him or his phone. It's a double-edged sword: a tracker would help us find him and also tell the SVR that he is worth tracking."

"Yeah, but I feel like I'm looking for a needle in a haystack. Do you have any idea what it's like to search for someone in the dark while dodging subway trains and strange people living underground? When I was a cop in California, we didn't have any underground places to worry about, so this is my first venture into such a place."

"When we're done with both cases, I'll arrange some CIA training in the DC Metro for you."

"I think the horse will be out of the barn at that point."

Sheila merely gave a ghost of a smile as Michelle disappeared from her office.

Michelle headed back to her train track in Russia, startling herself in that she landed in the alcove as a train was going past. The noise and light change made it a heart-pounding moment. Note to self, next time check the schedule before teleporting. If someone else had chosen the same alcove as Michelle, her body might have been thrown into the train.

Darkness resumed as she heard the train ahead braking. She took a few deep breaths while adjusting her night-vision goggles. One other piece of data that the analysts had located was the distance between stations. If Eric was choosing to escape some unknown threat via the train tracks, it made sense that he would choose the track that led him into a new station in the shortest distance. The average distance between stations was just over a mile, which under normal conditions was not a great distance to travel, but in this underworld, one had to constantly mark where a safe alcove was located so when the time came, you could jump into safety. That was assuming that the criminal element wasn't already there, but the analysts had also sent her a story about university students who explored the tunnels, sewers, and pipes and other infrastructure for the fun of it. They were called diggers and they wore knee-high boots to avoid getting wet. She supposed you needed that if you were traversing the sewer system, but while it was damp in the train tracks, there couldn't be knee-high water without affecting the trains.

Michelle was lost in her musings and recognized the sound of an oncoming train. Crap, she hadn't paid attention to where exactly she was and she moved around quickly before finding an empty alcove at the last minute. Whew. She could always have teleported home, but then she would have to start over at the last alcove to avoid getting hit by a train. It was better than being dead, but she wanted to explore these tracks and get out of Russia as soon as possible.

She paused for a quick text read that made her smile. Jason texted her saying it was quiet in Switzerland, and how was she doing?

She texted back that she was avoiding dying by subway car in a railroad tunnel. That wouldn't tell anyone what country or city she was located in, but it would give Jason a taste of her world.

Yuck.

Yep, that was a good summation of her feelings about this tunnel. She had at least half a mile to go to the next station and it was stressful looking at every stranger and sizing them up to be the missing agent, Eric.

He might be on this track, or he might have already made it to the next station. She had the advantage of the night-vision goggles to move quickly and safely and he might not have had them on his person when he went to meet his Russian contact. She had taken the track with the shortest distance to the next station, but he might have taken the other train line in the station or he might have gone forward of the station rather than behind, but that was farther away.

Again she heard the rumbling in the distance and looked for a place to stand safely. She found her alcove, but then noticed a struggle taking place on the tracks in front of her. She wouldn't have seen it but for her goggles. The first man had a backpack and a baseball cap similar to the one she had seen on Eric back at Langley. Still, the noise of the train was getting closer.

As she watched, the second man struck the first with a pipe and he crumbled to the ground and remained unmoving as he was stripped of his backpack and coat; the attacker then ran for the alcove. Michelle could feel the train bearing down on them and decided she couldn't let the man die. She ran full speed, flung herself on the ground and wrapped around him as the lights of the train car blinded her view with the goggles. One moment she could feel the wind and hear the screeching noise generated by the fast-approaching train and knew they were about to be crushed by the speeding train and the next moment she reveled in the dead silence in her living room.

She let go of the man, looked at his face for the first time, and was relieved to see it was Sheila's missing agent. She finally had a stroke of luck in that horrible Russian underground.

She called Sheila, "I have your missing agent in my living room. Where do you want him to go? He's injured. He was struck on the head with a pipe."

"Thank you, you can explain more later. Do you remember the hospital room of the unconscious man? Teleport the two of you to the empty bed in that room and I'll meet you there."

Michelle ended the call and did as Sheila asked. She removed her parka as she was overheating with both the adrenaline rush and the hospital room temperature. She waited inside the room for about fifteen minutes when Sheila arrived with a physician in tow. The unconscious man was unmoving and still comatose.

She told the physician what had happened with the pipe and backed away from the bed to give a fuller description to Sheila. There was blood on the sheet beneath the man's head. There was probably some on her living room floor.

The physician didn't ask how Michelle had arrived in the room with the agent, and for that she was grateful. She was also thrilled the man hadn't died as he was destined to do in seconds before she moved them home.

"I'm going to go home and clean up, then I'll head back to Switzerland. Can you let me know how he's doing?"

Sheila nodded and added, "Thank you, Michelle. Somehow, I knew you could find the needle in the haystack."

"Actually, if someone hadn't assaulted him in the underground, I'm not sure I would have noticed. All I knew was the train was coming and I couldn't let the man get hit by it."

"Were there many violent people in those underground tunnels?"

"No, he was the first person I saw endangered by someone else underground. There were people in the tunnel, but everyone kept to themselves. Do you think his attacker was someone from the SVR?"

"Maybe, but generally they want to take our spies alive so they can interrogate them or use them in a prisoner trade."

Michelle checked the hospital room; no one was watching, so she waved at Sheila and teleported home. She looked at the time in Basel and checked in with Jason. She texted a few times and got no response, which was odd. She grabbed a quick shower and left her Russian subway soiled clothes in her hamper to be washed. Feeling refreshed, she decided to check on him despite it being late evening, but the apartment was empty. She looked at the clock and decided it was unlikely that Jason was still out at dinner. Then she texted him again and heard the phone in another room of the apartment. Something was definitely wrong—Jason was missing. Then she looked around for the laptop. She would be able to see when he left the building by playing back the lobby camera information.

She quickly opened the program and found that Jason had left the apartment with two men about fifteen minutes before she'd arrived. They must have woken Jason out of sleep as it looked like he was wearing pajama bottoms under his coat. It didn't look like a friendly partnership heading to a bar to watch a game. She opened the feed for a second camera that looked at the street in front of the building. There was a car parked with a third man at the wheel. The two men got in the back seat and sandwiched

Jason in between them. Michelle made a copy of the footage and sent it to Sheila. She then zoomed in to find a license plate for identification. Then she put her coat on, grabbed a canister of pepper spray, and left the building. She headed the same direction as the car, hoping that she could catch up to it.

CHAPTER 14

She was moving from rooftop to rooftop, stopping only briefly to peer over the edge for the car. The night was dark, as was the car that Jason got into. Fortunately, she located the car as she could move faster than it despite the light traffic. That light traffic allowed her to spot the car just as it was getting close to one of the pharmaceutical companies. She saw the car park in front of a building they had surveilled before she went to Russia. She looked to see if the men had weapons in their hands, but she didn't see anything. The driver got out to lean against the car and smoke. Michelle knew she needed to pick them off one at a time. So she teleported in front of the smoker and sprayed his eyes. He immediately screamed and clutched his face.

His two friends turned around with Jason between them and she took both of them out in the same manner. She had three blinded men moaning in the front of the darkened building. She looked over at Jason.

"Are you okay?"

"Never better, let's go."

She teleported them home to their apartment and immediately

sent a text to Sheila saying that she had found and retrieved Jason and all was well in Switzerland.

"I didn't expect your help, but thanks," said Jason. "How did you find me?"

"I finished my Russian assignment and texted you and got no response. So I came here and the apartment was dark and your cell phone was here, so I knew you were in trouble. I remembered to open up the laptop and look for surveillance video. I found you being escorted from the building by two thugs and pushed into a car in your pajama bottoms. I grabbed some pepper spray and went roof hopping looking for the car. Fortunately, there isn't much traffic after midnight in Basel. I searched in the right direction, and I caught up to you. I couldn't tell if the men were armed, but I decided to surprise them with pepper spray. Voila, you're back here ready for bed. How did the men get in?"

"Oldest trick in the book—maintenance. One guy said there was a building emergency that had been caught by their sensors at their building management headquarters. I needed to let him in to check for carbon dioxide as that was the sensor that was alarming. It sounded serious so when I unlocked the door, I found two men holding handguns on me. I decided to go peacefully and see what they were up to."

"I was tempted to see what they were up to as well, but given the ketamine and potassium that we have come across in this case, I didn't want to risk your life. I let Sheila know that you were missing and I was searching for you. Then I texted her that I found you and we're safely back home. You may want to drop her a detailed email about the event. Man, I'm tired. I've rescued two men in the last six hours or so, and the adrenaline rush of that has left me exhausted. I don't know how Wonder Woman does her job. See you in the morning."

Before she left their living room, Jason said, "Thanks, Michelle. You saved me from a beating at the very least and probably much worse. Sweet dreams."

She was sitting with Jason at breakfast the next morning going over the case. Overnight, she received an email from Sheila with the information that Eric had a brain bleed and a concussion but had recovered consciousness and would in time make a full recovery. He couldn't remember how he got out of the train track tunnel or even Russia, but was grateful to be back in the United States. The physician informed the agent it was likely he would never recover the memory. Michelle certainly hoped that he would never remember the pain of the strike and the terror of nearly being run over by a train. She admitted to herself that to know she had single-handedly saved a fellow CIA agent from certain death felt really good. Sheila also acknowledged their adventures of the night before and had little comment.

"So what did you do in my absence besides get kidnapped?"

"Seriously? While you were out saving another agent's life, I was at a local pub watching people in Basel hang out. Then I came home and went to bed, got kidnapped, got rescued, went to bed a second time. It was hard work, but someone has to do it."

"Actually, you had a role in saving that agent's life."

"I did? How? I wasn't there."

"It was the teleporting practice with you in Venezuela that gave me the confidence to know how, with very little time, I could wrap myself around the other agent and get us both out of there. You are the only other human in the world that I've moved. Well, let me correct that as now I've moved my children, but seriously the practice we did in Venezuela and understanding what does and doesn't work gave me the confidence to try."

"Did you know it was the agent Sheila was looking for?"

"No, it was dark, and I had night-vision goggles and I just felt bad about this person getting a pipe to the head. I remember thinking that I hadn't seen any violence despite the creepiness of walking around in the dark, dodging trains. I quickly lay down as the train was bearing down on us and took the man to my living room floor. Once there I could see the face of my rescued person and it was the agent. So, I called Sheila and she directed me to move him to a hospital bed. It would have been a real tragedy for him and his family if he had been run over by the train. He likely would have been buried in an unmarked grave in Russia or eaten by the tunnel rats. No one would ever have known what happened to him."

"Yikes. You've really put your life on the line a few times for the agency. Sheila must be grateful you accidentally found her agent and that she doesn't have to contend with explaining to a random Russian citizen how he ended up in the United States. It's also convenient that the man was unconscious when you brought him home, so they can make up any story about how he got here."

"Yes. So we're back to spying on our pharmaceutical company today and seeing if we can cause anything new to happen," Michelle said.

"Neither I nor the agency has come up with any other ideas to see what is afoot. Since the American company staff is in protective custody, there's no activity there and we still don't know who was behind those murders."

The weather was cool but dry, so they took up their positions near the pharmaceutical company in question. It was the only way they could think of to stir the pot. They spent an uneventful morning, went to lunch, and then returned for more surveillance.

"I know that a fair number of private detectives do mind-numbing surveillance like we're doing, but I just have to say that I would really like a level of excitement somewhere between nearly being crushed by a subway car and my eyeballs falling out in boredom watching the building in Basel, Switzerland."

"I hear you, but we're going to have to keep this up a while longer. Let's meander slowly home and hope that we pick up a tail. If we don't, we'll try again tomorrow. Look at the bright side, we're not conducting this surveillance in China. If we were in that country, we likely would've likely been harassed by the police and told to move along."

"Maybe the Chinese and the Swiss are collaborating to stop our American company with its market-changing product from being developed," Michelle suggested.

"Maybe. If we were following that line of thought, we would try to get a picture of anyone of Asian heritage entering the Swiss building. I visited the websites of the large Chinese pharmaceutical companies, and their leadership, based on their pictures and their names, were all of Chinese heritage. Likewise, the Swiss companies featured European names. I'm stereotyping the situation I'm sure, but we run with probabilities and those are the probabilities in this case."

"It's an idea worth exploring. Have you seen the weather for tomorrow? Will we be out front watching the company?"

"No rain, so we'll be out front. Have you noticed that we are being followed?"

"No. You know me; I rarely notice my surroundings. My mind was on China and Switzerland. Who is following us, and should we do anything about it?"

"Let's keep walking so they know where we're staying. We wanted something to happen, and this is our opportunity. At the moment it's a single man who's following us. I haven't seen the woman from the bar a few nights ago on our tail or even close to the building that we've been surveilling."

"We could tackle him and see if he has any weapons."

"We don't want to come to the attention of Swiss authorities and that might do it. People have guns in Switzerland as it's a hunting population. What we could do is this: we make a turn at the next corner and you could teleport behind the guy once we're out of his line of sight. If you make some noise behind him so that he sees you, that should freak him out and cause some action. However, that might cause some bad action, so scratch that idea."

"Actually I like that idea. This is a fairly public area with cars going by and people occasionally on the street. I can't imagine this guy's going to turn around and fire at me."

They made the turn, and Michelle did as planned with a quick stop at the top of the building to make sure there was no one behind the man whom she would startle. She would be the only pedestrian to unnerve him. She moved close to him and then coughed just to make sure he knew there was a person behind them. He looked over her shoulder and then quickly whipped his head around the second time as though to confirm what he saw. He moved his head so quickly Michelle was worried he would strain a muscle and have his head stuck in a sideways position. She smiled at that thought and at him.

She said good evening to him in German and then walked by him as though she had somewhere to be. She quickly caught up to Jason around the next corner as he'd slowed his pace waiting to see what happened. The man had slowed down and seemed to stop following them.

"Rats, that wasn't the reaction I was hoping for. I'm afraid we're in for another day of boring surveillance unless someone else gets on our tail in the next few minutes."

"Still, it was rather fun to shake the man up. I need to get my jollies where I can, and this was a funny moment. When I was in college, I fell asleep in front of a blowing fan and woke up with a stiff neck. I couldn't turn my head back to the center. It took a week of muscle relaxants before I could move it back to the center again. He whipped his head around so quickly to look at me I thought his neck might get stuck looking to the side, but he turned back to the center so apparently there was no muscle tightness on his part. Look on the bright side, at least something happened last night and this afternoon and maybe it will bring more activity tonight or tomorrow. Do you want to stay in the apartment and cook something for dinner, or do you want to go out and see if we can stir up trouble in a pub?"

"Let's stay in. It's more relaxing and I can have something besides German sausage for dinner. Maybe we'll luck out with a visit from someone trying to scope out the apartment."

"We've had seven alerts this past hour. Fortunately, most of them stopped at the mailbox and we can conclude that they live here. If I understood IT and in particular facial recognition better, we could program those cameras to not activate for residents in this building. Alas, I don't have that expertise," Jason said.

"Are we worried about our personal safety, or are we curious about who's trying to follow us?"

"I'm not worried about our personal safety, are you? I now know not to open the door to maintenance."

"No. Why don't we change these camera notifications, so we don't get an alert every time someone passes them and instead make it a practice to go online and check the cameras every one to two hours?"

Jason thought about Michelle's suggestion and nodded. He went to the software and made the changes. Except for checking the cameras, they had a quiet night and the next day prepared for more boring surveillance.

CHAPTER 15

*S*heila texted them after they had been at their surveillance spot for a few hours.

Man at lunch the other day identified as the grandson of the Swiss company founder and is the current CEO. The Australian pharmacy chain representative was just a cover.

Any idea where he is now? Michelle texted back.

No.

"Well, that's interesting. So, the newly identified grandson didn't walk to the restaurant with the other man from this building. Why?"

"There are numerous good reasons for that—maybe he was away from the headquarters to attend a meeting in town and needed to meet the guy for lunch. What's his name?"

"Sheila says it is Noah Schmid."

"Where did Noah really go on the airplane? He was headed to Singapore, but was that his final destination? I'll ask that Sheila have the analysts or hackers or someone track him down."

"So this is interesting. We have one guy who's a low-level criminal carrying around injectors, a grandson of a pharmaceutical company founder trying to hide behind the cover of an

Australian pharmaceutical rep, and a woman whose role we don't understand yet are all who have made contact with us. Also, the three men who kidnapped you. Did I leave anyone out?" Michelle asked.

"There was the man from last evening who was following us."

"I feel so much better now that we have all these characters in play. At least something's happening here even though the days feel boring."

"I've had cases like this before that seem to be a very slow burn. The good news is we've come to the attention of someone who's involved with something nefarious. I think this activity goes beyond what the average company might do about the theft of trade secrets," Jason said.

"I think our next steps are to identify our two unknown people—the man and the woman—while the agency goes about locating the CEO's present location. I'm also curious as to whether he was in San Francisco. Of course, he didn't have to be the actual hitman. Whoever is behind all this activity has proven that they don't mind hiring a criminal to stab you with potassium."

"Indeed. I wonder what's taking the agency so long to identify the woman? It's had her picture for like thirty-six hours now."

"Maybe she was wearing a disguise. Maybe our picture wasn't good enough. Maybe as a Swiss citizen her face hasn't ended up in any kind of artificial intelligence yet. Jason, you're starting to sound impatient like me."

"Let's go to lunch nearby and walk slowly in hopes that someone will follow us," Jason suggested.

"Sounds as good a plan as anything."

For the remainder of the day and into the evening, Jason and Michelle failed to locate anyone who was potentially following them. They had dinner in their apartment and called it an early night.

They were woken up by the sound of breaking glass. They

were both out of their beds meeting in the little alcove that contained the doors to their bedrooms. There was silence again except a hissing sound.

"Sounds like gas is being released. I wonder what kind?" Michelle said.

"Let's not take any chances. Gather up some clothes, shoes, and a jacket and then maybe you could teleport us to the roof."

"Why the roof?"

"I think someone might be waiting for us to leave the building and we don't want to get in their crosshairs."

They took a few seconds to do as planned and then Michelle took the two of them to the roof. As it was early evening at Langley, Jason called Sheila with the news of the glass breakage, while Michelle searched the ground for the person who broke their window. She saw shadows moving, and Michelle gave chase from her rooftop perch. The two shadows slipped into a car and took off. Michelle could have followed them, but she had no backup. Instead, she teleported ahead to the first intersection and leaned out to take a picture of the car and its occupants. She dropped her phone back in her coat pocket and teleported back to the roof. Jason was still on the phone with Sheila. They weren't calling the agency because they were in danger; rather they needed the gas canister evaluated and then the apartment would get cold with the big window cracked. They needed to stay away from the notice of Swiss authorities.

Michelle took them both back to Virginia, then she fetched a hazmat suit and breathing apparatus from Sheila's office and returned to the apartment to collect an air sample and bag the smoky device. She returned to the CIA and gave Sheila the sealed samples to process. Then she called Jason and made plans to teleport back to the apartment in the morning. They left a message with the apartment management about the window breakage and the fact that they had moved into a hotel for the evening and would meet the landlord in the morning to discuss the repair. The

CIA rented the building under the front of a U.S. business and Jason and Michelle were just the employees who happened to occupy the apartment at the time of the window breakage.

By the next morning, anyone on the street could see the broken window. Other tenants in the building asked them questions as they walked into the building. They got beyond that, had a meeting with the management company, and they gave their information to the police for a report for the management company's insurance provider. The police were very puzzled by the broken window as it was something that didn't happen in Basel. Fortunately, Sheila had provided them with another device to place in their apartment as evidence for the Swiss police to collect. It was a European smoke bomb, so that covered all the bases of the police investigation.

The analysts at the agency were still working on identifying the maker of the original bomb and enhancing the photo Michelle took of the getaway car. The gas inside the bomb was identified as carbon monoxide gas.

"Back to our building?" Jason said, mid-morning after everyone had cleared out. The window was already replaced.

"Yes, they may be wondering if we're still alive."

"There is that."

"Maybe we'll run into the woman again. I sure would like to know who she is."

"If she had a disguise on, she may have already walked past us and we didn't recognize her."

"True. It's been an eventful twelve hours. Although to be fair to the surveillance gods, I did mention that watching these buildings was boring, and I was looking for action. I hope we get a decent night's sleep tonight."

"Well, you wanted excitement in Switzerland, so your wishes are being fulfilled," Jason said.

"Looks like I'm getting my other wish. Is that woman who is walking toward us the same one from the pub?"

"I do believe you're correct. I wonder what she's going to say to us."

Instead, she didn't approach them, but walked right by them and headed down the street.

"Well, that's interesting. She could have indeed been distracted and not seen the two of us here, but after all the staring she did the other night, I find that hard to believe," Jason said.

"Yes. Perhaps this is our signal to split up. Do you want to follow her or should I?"

"You, in case she heads in somewhere that men are not allowed, like the bathroom."

"Okay, good luck with something interesting happening on your end."

Michelle followed the woman down the street and around the corner. As she turned the corner, two men reached out to grab her. She slipped their hands and teleported backward a good twenty feet. The men looked dumbfounded as they were sure she was in their grasp. Then she made eye contact with the pub woman, who was clearly expecting that she would be detained.

"Who are you?" Michelle asked the woman. The two men began charging her, so she simply moved so that she was in the mysterious woman's face.

"Who are you?" she repeated.

The woman said something to the men in what she thought might be German and they began moving back toward her. So Michelle moved across the street and said, "Look, I'm a former Olympian in running short distances. I will continue to move faster than your men."

The road had occasional vehicle traffic, but it wasn't well traveled with either cars or pedestrians. There were apartment buildings lining both sides of the street and since it was nearly midday, no one was leaving or returning from work or school.

The woman looked dumbfounded and confused. How did Michelle move so fast and why wasn't she being detained by her goons? They tried a third time and couldn't capture the American woman. Finally, the woman nodded her head at the men as though to say go away, and they did.

Michelle moved back across the street to talk with the woman.

"What's your name?" She repeated for what felt like the umpteenth time. She wondered if the woman would finally tell Michelle her name.

"It doesn't matter," she said, turning around and walking down the street.

It was Michelle's turn to be dumbfounded—should she follow the unknown woman or give up on her? She was close to being caught on camera with her teleportation skill, so she decided to cool it and not follow her. She turned and walked back to Jason's position.

"Well?"

CHAPTER 16

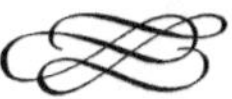

"She wanted one or both of us to follow her as she had two men who tried to take me into custody the moment she rounded a street corner."

"I'm thinking that plan didn't succeed since you're standing in front of me."

"Damn straight it didn't work. Our girl hadn't expected that outcome and after three attempts to capture me, she sent the men away and simply walked away. I debated following her, but I think we'll see her again since she elaborately planned to try and capture one or both of us."

"Good thing you followed, as I might have busted a few noses in my evasion of these guys."

"Have you evaded two men before?" Michelle asked, curious about his past as a case officer.

"Yes. The CIA teaches its new entrants a bunch of different skills, or at least they used to. I don't know what's in the training curriculum now. I've been in a few dicey situations wherein I've taken two men on. Fortunately, they have been unarmed—no knife or gun—and so I've won my fist fights."

"They teach self-defense at the police academy, but that was eons ago. It's much easier to evade. I told this twosome that I was an Olympian in short distances, and they would never catch me. Then I teleported five feet at a time in quick succession, so it looked like someone was running."

"That's a smart way to play down your special skills."

"The first time you hear an explanation of my skill, you don't believe it because there is no such thing as magic, right? But moving in five-feet increments, it's a plausible explanation as long as you don't see me in slow motion on a tape. If someone did, they would find that my feet aren't moving fast enough to cover the ground that I've crossed."

"Interesting. So what's our game plan now?" Jason asked.

"I did grab a picture of the two goons at one point, so we can feed that to the analysts if it is any good. Just a moment," Michelle said, pulling out her phone to look at the picture. Then she nodded, the picture was doable. "I suspect it will come back that they are Swiss or German low-life criminals, and they were hired. The woman didn't tell me her name, but she did come out of the building we've been surveilling. She must have some connection to it. I think we should head back to our apartment and do some online research on the company. I know the analysts have already done so, but we're on the ground here. We've seen her exit that building several times. She has some relationship to that company."

"I don't have a better suggestion. I wonder if our glass will be broken again. Hopefully they recognize that didn't work. I know you got a look at the two men last night—were they the same men? At least by height and weight? I realize you couldn't see them very well in the dark."

Michelle paused to think about what she had seen and finally said, "I'm not sure."

Jason shrugged and they walked back to their apartment without anyone following them. They ate in their apartment for a third night and spent their evening looking for any odd mention of the company and its employees. Had those employees lectured at the local university, or at local civic organizations? Had they received a medal from their country's leader for education or business acumen? They finally found the woman in the society pages where she was listed and pictured at a friend's wedding.

"I found her. Her name is Sabrina Müller. It's a common last name in this country, so there may be more than one person in Switzerland with her name, but she appears to also be a grand-child of the founder. She and Noah Schmid are cousins. So did she or Noah concoct the idea to try and attack us?"

"Good question. I'm going to go with her as she seems the bolder of the two cousins. Let's find what role she plays for the company and whether either cousin was in San Francisco."

"Do you still have the spreadsheet with the conference attendees?"

"Gee whiz, I forgot I borrowed that list."

"Borrowed? That implies you have plans to give it back."

"Yes, . . . well no. I won't be giving it back. Maybe the proper word is I copied the list from the organizers of the conference. So what do we do with this information? I wonder who they think we're working for. I mean, we know we're working for the U.S. government, but do they know that?" Michelle took a moment to scan the attendance list for the convention and did not find the cousins as registered participants for the conference.

"If the CIA has been good with our constructed covers, then they should see us as potential competitors in the pharmaceutical field. Though if they saw us outside of their building, they have to wonder how we have time to sit there."

"True . . . ," Michelle said, thinking. "If they are behind the attacks on us, then they certainly could have ordered the murders in San Francisco. Even if they looked guilty, what would the agency do about it? I mean, this is Switzerland; we don't have any authority here and we haven't collected any information other than suspicion about their connection to murders in California."

"We do have recent evidence, and it's time for another call with Sheila. I'd like to know what was in those bags you dropped off with her. Will these bags reveal something as bad as the potassium in that syringe? If so, we're not taking the dangers of Switzerland seriously enough. The surveillance may be boring, but the action that comes our way is deadly."

They were soon on an encrypted video call with Sheila.

"I was about to call you two to relay new information. We were able to track Noah Schmid beyond Singapore. He changed planes and arrived at Guangdong. So we may have a partnership between the Swiss and the Chinese. We also got the samples back on the smoke canister and those bastards were out to kill you two. We confirmed that the smoke canister was filled with carbon monoxide gas. It was likely easy to acquire, and given the layout of your apartment they were trying to make you run through the gas in order to evacuate the apartment. The carbon monoxide gas is common and so we can't blame any particular country or even a terrorist group over it, as it's far too common. You're making somebody nervous in Switzerland. I also think you've rattled enough cages there; you can move on and rattle some cages back in China."

"Before I forget, we identified the woman we've been interacting with. She is Noah Schmid's cousin. Her name is Sabrina Müller," Jason said.

"Do you have someone else you can send? As Caucasians we stand out in China and are easy targets for the police. What can you do to change that?" Michelle asked.

"I have the agency's Chinese-speaking case officers deployed elsewhere. You do realize that yours is not the only case in that country, and that China is a threat to the security of the United States?"

"Yeah, I get that, and I suppose our lab company affects thousands of people with cancer, whereas the security of the United States threatens millions of people. At the risk of offending any

Asian employees of the agency, is there anyone in our special effects department who could help both of us with make-up to make us look closer to being Asian?"

"Actually, we do have someone who can help you. Why don't you plan on coming back to base and we'll see what our special effects people can do to make you feel more comfortable in China. I know we can fit you with an earpiece so you can better understand the language spoken around you. We'll have to limit it to Cantonese as that is the main language in that region. If someone is speaking Mandarin near you, it will confuse the listening device, so you still won't understand Mandarin or some of the other Chinese dialects spoken near you."

"Okay. Are we flying or teleporting home?" Michelle asked.

"Flying. Your plane departs early tomorrow morning. I'll send the ticket information. It's always good to leave a country with a record trail."

"When do we leave for China?" Jason asked.

"The next day. You'll arrive here before midday and that will give us the afternoon to teach you how to transform yourselves. Then you'll depart for Guangdong," Sheila said.

"Do you have an official residence for us this time so we don't run into problems with the landlord?" Jason asked.

"Of course; you're staying at a hotel. There may or may not be more eyes on you there, but then again, there are cameras everywhere so there is no use trying to escape them. You'll be Chinese Americans who speak English only."

"Okay, see you tomorrow," Michelle said.

They ended the call and looked at each other.

"My body is going to be confused by all these time zone changes. I'll have to think I'm in Swiss time while home, and then China is just six hours ahead. Geez, how do pilots handle moving among all these time zones?" Michelle asked.

"Your body is confused because it has spent time in three different time zones in the last thirty-six hours and it's about to spend it in three more time zones over the next thirty-six hours."

"On that note, we should pack and try to sleep. I see from Sheila's email that we have to be at the airport in about six hours. She has a taxi picking us up at four in the morning. Ugh. At least she booked us in business class so we can try and get some sleep."

"These assignments seem to play havoc with our sleep. In Venezuela it was too hot to sleep. Now we're on the move so much, we don't have time to get proper rest. Oh well, it will get better. She's booked us into a nice hotel in China, so maybe we can start by catching up on our sleep there."

"That will depend on how good our cover is. I'm anxious to see myself made into an ethnic Chinese. Both of us will have to have our hair dyed black for starters, but I guess we'll see how it's done tomorrow. I'm going to go pack. We still have a fair amount of food here for the landlord to take care of, but I would think they would be glad to see us go."

Jason nodded and they set out to make the apartment ready for their departure. Jason also took time to remove the cameras they had set up in the lobby. It would not be good for those to be discovered.

The next day after the long flight home, they were in a lab inside Langley with a make-up artist working on their appearance. They were both amazed with their appearance once the artist was done. They added a tint dye overall to their skin like a tanning booth set-up. Their hair and eyebrows were dyed black, and semi-permanent make-up was applied, and they were taught how to keep it refreshed. They had new photos taken for new passports and were ready to leave on the long journey back to Guangdong.

CHAPTER 17

They were able to catch up on sleep given their comfortable plane seats, but it was hard not to have one's body confused by what time of day it was.

As they walked through immigration, everything went smoothly. The customs agents spoke in Cantonese, and he frowned at them when they replied in English. Apparently, he didn't like the fact that they were of Chinese heritage yet didn't speak the language. That was according to what he said, and their earpieces translated. Instead, they both smiled and shrugged and Michelle said in English, "We hope to pick up a few words of Mandarin while we're here. I think that is the language my grandparents spoke."

"Cantonese is the language of this region if this is where your family is from."

"It is. So, I'll work on Cantonese. Thank you."

Without further interaction they reached the exit, entered a taxi, and gave the driver the address of their hotel. They had made a similar journey a little more than a week ago. Michelle tried to remember the day of the week that they had first entered China, and she decided it was actually two weeks since they had last been in this city.

In the event the taxi was bugged or the driver was an agent, Jason asked Michelle, "Are any of your relatives living close to our hotel?"

It took Michelle a minute before she remembered their cover. "No, they are farmers and I see no farms inside the cities. How about your family?"

"They are not near the hotel either. I looked up the city of my grandfather's birth and it is at least two-hundred miles from here. He's lost contact with his family and advises me not to bother searching for them here."

Michelle was about to answer Jason keeping up their cover story, but they had reached their hotel and they bailed out of the taxi and grabbed their luggage. It was just after noon Guangdong time and early for check-in, but the agency had purchased an early check-in. They weren't tired so much as desiring a shower after all the airplane air. They scanned their room for any cameras or listening devices and found none, so they relaxed in the luxury hotel room.

An hour later, refreshed, they set out to stake out the original pharmaceutical company. The agency had continued to monitor conversations from the listening devices Michelle and Jason placed, but nothing of any significance had surfaced. They slowly made their way from the park up to the street where the pharmaceutical giant was located, watching the activity for a while.

"I have to tell you that this is freaky. I feel like I'm standing out as a Caucasian, then I'll catch my reflection somewhere and realize I look like almost anybody else in this city. Our hearing aids are helpful also, as we can understand most of the conversations around us," Michelle said.

"Yes, it is a good disguise. I've been thinking about Noah Schmid. He arrived in China at least four days ago. He may have left by now. I would think the agency is monitoring his movements, but maybe not. I wonder if we could spot him going into this building or just being in the neighborhood here through facial recognition."

"Your suggestion sounds plausible to me. Where would you stick a camera in this area to track that?"

"Would you be able to hang one on one of the sides of the building? It would be easy to teleport here at night and adhere it with double-sided tape."

"I could do that, but I would worry that the rain would cause it to peel off and it would drop on someone below. That would blow our cover."

"We'll let the technical people figure that one out," Jason said.

A text to Sheila was responded to with a teleport request in three hours for Michelle to pick up the camera and glue. Michelle picked up the gear and later that night, she stuck cameras on a few buildings in the area around the pharmaceutical company. The agency gave her software so she could check the focus of each camera before moving on to the next one.

The agency was unable to find a return flight yet for Noah Schmid, so he might still be in the area. Meanwhile, Michelle and Jason explored Shenzhen and Guangzhou, which were the two largest cities within the province that contained a lot of pharmaceutical companies. The province was huge, with over a hundred million people living there. There was noise and traffic and hustle and bustle typical of any highly populated city.

"I'll admit that I'm enjoying walking around every day exploring this large metropolitan area, but we're not making much forward progress on the case. The likelihood of us randomly running into Noah Schmid is very low," Michelle said.

"I agree with you, but we have to keep up the surveillance. We can only hope that our suspect is caught on camera. Otherwise, this just happens to be a grand vacation on the agency's expense account."

No sooner were they lamenting their boredom with this case

than the agency sent a text indicating they had located Noah Schmid on camera going into a particular building. Sheila wanted Michelle to use her teleportation skills to drop transmitters into Noah's clothing. She teleported atop the building in the neighborhood where Noah had been spotted. She located a street-level location she could teleport to and she did so, sending her information to Jason who was arriving by taxi. She could've teleported him with her, but she was going into an unknown area and might have to move fast. She didn't like to worry about properly enclosing Jason with her arms and legs to successfully teleport him with her.

The agency texted a picture of Noah and she looked around for their suspect. She spotted him getting into a taxi and sent off a text to Jason telling him to stay where he was as their suspect was on the move. She then began following the taxi from a series of rooftops. As the traffic was congested, it wasn't that hard to follow the taxi. Taxis had a unique paint job and that made it easier to follow one down the street. It took him toward the Pearl River and the many luxury hotels lining that area. It deposited their suspect at a well-known international hotel chain. She texted that information to Jason and Sheila. Then she teleported to the ground near the hotel and looked around for a place to wait for Jason to join her or for their suspect to be on the move again. Teleporting in this congested city of millions of people was no easy feat.

Fortunately, the Pearl River was scenic and a popular location to take pictures. Michelle found a place to wait for Jason to arrive and to observe the hotel entrance without looking suspicious. Jason showed up in fifteen minutes.

"In some ways, I make a difficult case officer to be paired with. I can take off and chase a suspect leaving you behind and out of the action. Sorry about that," Michelle said.

"True. However, we're a more effective team in that you've got the speed to follow a suspect and then I can catch up and we have two sets of eyes to determine our suspect's actions. Besides, you're the safest case officer I could be paired with. If the going gets tough, then you can teleport us out of the gunfight."

"True. There's a positive way to look at the situation," Michelle said, holding out her hand for a fist bump.

They settled in to watch the hotel's entrance. As the day wore on, they didn't see their suspect leave, but they did see Sabrina Müller arrive.

"Well, that's interesting. If she is here, then the two cousins are colluding about something. We need to understand her role in the company. She's not listed in the Board of Directors or in the management of the company, so what exactly is she in China to do?" Jason mused.

"I wonder if they are considering a merger of the two companies. The Chinese one is bigger, but the Swiss company is very old school. Perhaps it has some intellectual property of value."

"More research for the analysts. I guess we should get cameras aimed at that hotel. To track these two."

"I'd rather teleport into their hotel rooms and place trackers in clothing, briefcases, and purses. Then we can really track where they are going. I'll ask the analysts to find the hotel rooms for these two, so I can place trackers," Michelle said.

"Should we move to a hotel closer to this one?"

"Not necessarily, I can always teleport us back and forth between this hotel and ours."

"I'd rather not stay in our suspects' hotel anyway."

"You forget that while we've met them, our features have changed, so hopefully we aren't recognizable on sight."

"True, but I'd also like not to come to the attention of Chinese authorities. I don't know if they track when non-citizens change hotels," Jason said.

"Yeah, that's true. Of course, this isn't a great tourist destination in China. It's not like the Great Wall or the Terracotta Warriors are in the vicinity. We could take a day trip to Hong

Kong or Macau and then teleport back here to watch our subjects. Of course, we might lose them while we were in transit to these other locations, but if I can get trackers on them, then we're home free. I bet the analysts will have their hotel room numbers for us by later tonight. If I must, I can enter their hotel rooms while they're asleep and place trackers.

"On that note, should we wrap it up here and return to our hotel? I must say I love our make-up jobs and I'm so much more relaxed in China this time knowing that at least on the surface I don't stick out." Michelle said.

"Yes, let's return and I agree you seem more relaxed even though this is just our second day here," Jason said.

They had a quiet dinner while they waited for the agency to tell them which hotel rooms the cousins were in. Meanwhile Michelle found a picture of the hotel's rooms, so she knew where to teleport to inside the room. Finally, at close to ten in the evening, they got word of the hotel room numbers the cousins were assigned. They weren't located on the same floor, but then, Sabrina arrived several days after Noah. Maybe they hadn't asked to be close by.

Michelle planned to teleport to just inside the hallway door to one of the rooms. That way if the occupant was awake and watching TV, they wouldn't see her. She had six trackers in her pocket to drop into jacket pockets, purses, or briefcases. She set her alarm for just before midnight and Jason was awake awaiting her return. She had a weak flashlight in case she needed it and then she was ready.

"You seem like the modern version of a case officer. In the old days, we had to use a series of picks to break into a room and place trackers. Now you just teleport to the room."

"Fingers crossed nothing goes wrong," Michelle said before disappearing. Before he had time to move, she was back.

"What happened?"

"There were other men in the hotel room beating up Noah

Schmidt. At least I think that Noah was likely the one being slugged. Should we interfere?"

Jason thought for a while then said, "I can't imagine they plan to kill him; maybe he is being roughed up. For all the sins of China, they don't routinely murder foreign nationals. Still, this case could be the exception. Did anyone see you?"

"No, they were near the window, the lighting was dim, and no one was looking at the hotel door. I wonder if they will go after Sabrina next?"

"We still need those trackers placed. Why don't you try her room?"

Michelle nodded and took a little more time returning this time. The delay gave Jason time to worry about what was happening in Sabrina's room. Just about the time he talked himself into the explanation that she could take care of herself, she reappeared in their hotel room.

"How did it go?"

"It was quiet in the room. I don't know if Sabrina was in bed and asleep or if she was out of the room. Still, I found a jacket, a purse, and a suitcase in which I placed trackers. So it was uneventful. What should we do about Noah? If he was beaten badly, he could be unconscious. Or he could've turned the lights on in his hotel room to see what was going on with his wounds. Or he could be dead."

"I would vote that we wait an hour, then try his room again," Jason said.

"What if he's dead or severely injured? Should I check on him?"

"Good question. You don't want to alert him to your presence in his room. How 'bout if you teleport there with a wig and a surgical mask. That would disguise your features."

"And if I sense him needing medical care?"

"I would call the hotel operator and tell them there's a medical emergency inside the room. I'd put something in the door to hold it open, perhaps turn the room lights on or at least some of them and get the heck out of there. Of course, I would plant a few devices before I left."

Michelle wore gloves when she was planting any kind of device for the CIA, so they didn't need to worry about her fingerprints being left behind. She looked at her watch and then set her phone timer for forty-five minutes.

"Why do you think they were beating up Noah? It's not like street thugs would get past the front desk up to his room. This has to be targeted. I would think that the beating is being used as encouragement for him to do something. The question is what?" Jason said.

"That's a good question. They already made attempts on the lives of the American company employees and they are now out of reach. So maybe he hasn't paid his share of the assassin's fees. I'm not that good about figuring out criminal motives. We should pass this on to the agency and let them figure it out."

"You mean in all your years as a cop, you never tried to figure out the people you were arresting?"

"I might've done that my rookie year and then I realized I might never understand the criminal mind. For many people it was sheer laziness that they couldn't figure out any other way to get money or supplies other than to take it from someone else. That works for them until they get caught. Something deeper is going on here, though."

They continued to speculate and then Michelle's timer rang. She put gloves on, checked her pockets for the tracking devices, and gave Jason a fist bump for good luck and she teleported into Noah Schmid's hotel room.

The room was dark and quiet. Michelle waited for her eyes to adapt to the dark and looked around the hotel room. Between the curtains there was light shining through from nearby buildings. This Chinese city had a lot of ambient light at night. You couldn't see the stars in the sky. She looked around for Noah and saw him slumped on the floor. She quietly approached and listened again. Was he dead? She looked at his body to see if there were noticeable injuries— was there blood trickling from anywhere or any limbs at odd angles? The light wasn't good enough to give her answers. She risked leaning over the man and searching for a pulse. She found one and decided she would go the route of reporting a medical emergency. The fact that he hadn't woken up when she touched his skin suggested he was unconscious. She went to the bathroom and found a hotel phone and called the operator to report a medical emergency. She dropped a few of the trackers into his stuff and put a towel in the doorway to block it open. Then she left and returned to Jason and their hotel a few miles away.

CHAPTER 18

"I think Noah was unconscious as he didn't respond when I searched for a pulse. I left a few trackers in his stuff and medical help should be arriving. I left a towel in the door, so they don't have to knock. I might teleport to the outside of his hotel and see if an ambulance pulls up to it."

"That's a good idea. Call me and tell me what you see, or if the area is empty of people, come back to the room and teleport me back with you."

Michelle nodded and was gone. She teleported to the space where she and Jason had watched the hotel earlier. There were still people around but not nearly as many as there were during the daytime hours. Still, she watched a little and decided not to risk teleporting and then returning with Jason. She called him on the cell to chat about what she was seeing. Then she heard sirens in the distance that seemed to be getting closer. An ambulance and a couple of police cars arrived at the same time to the hotel's entrance. As Michelle watched, an empty stretcher was unloaded, and they followed the police upstairs. She moved closer and saw one policeman move toward the registration area presumably to talk to the hotel operator that had taken Michelle's call. She would be remembered for her English and the operator might have identified her as American. The police would wonder about the injured Swiss man and the American woman who was nowhere to be found. She bet the police would pull hallway tapes. Depending on where the cameras were located, they might catch the door opening and her placing a towel in it, but she had stayed well behind the door when she placed the towel, so there should be no record of her face.

About ten minutes later, the stretcher returned with someone on it. She wasn't close enough to see a face on the stretcher. It was also not clear if he was conscious, but they loaded him into an ambulance and took off. One police car followed, and another stayed behind at the hotel. There was nothing more for her to do here other than to see if someone figured out Noah's connection to Sabrina and wait and see if she departed the hotel for presumably the hospital. However, it would likely take the police a little longer to make that connection. They might even suspect Sabrina of making the call to the hotel operator.

She returned to the room she was sharing with Jason and relayed what she saw, and updated Sheila with an email. They decided there was nothing more to do that night except get some sleep.

The next morning, they checked their GPS trackers. Sabrina Müller's tracker showed her visiting a Chinese hospital. Whether Chinese authorities made the connection or if his family back home in Switzerland alerted Sabrina was unclear.

"We seem to be at a standstill. We can't get in to talk to Noah. Spying on a Chinese company isn't likely to be fruitful. So that leaves Sabrina. Should we approach her and see if we can find out what's up?" Michelle asked.

"Yes, let's approach her. We know she's in this up to her elbows since she tried to have us harmed or killed in Basel. She's not in her country and I suspect she's feeling vulnerable with Noah in the hospital. Where should we corner her? I think the hotel room would be the best choice, but then how do we access her room? In our hotel, you need your room key to operate the elevator."

"We could head to the hospital now and corner her there."

"I like that idea. She'll hopefully be vulnerable with her cousin in the hospital," Jason said.

"We can only hope. She did hire a few idiot criminals to take us out, but maybe the Chinese got her attention. If Noah is unconscious at this point, he likely has some serious brain damage. She loses her partner in crime; she's all alone here and could be the next person beaten up. She's likely not the person who is going to take over the company from what we've seen with their Board of Directors. She only has the power that Noah gives her in regard to the company," Michelle said.

"Okay, let's take a taxi to the hospital and see what's happening. I looked it up on the internet and it's huge, so I'm not sure if we'll be able to randomly come across Sabrina."

They took a taxi to the hospital and walked around. It was indeed large. It was twice the size of Johns Hopkins Medical Center, which they both had thought was a large campus. They entered the lobby and decided it was hopeless to accidentally come across Sabrina. They watched the GPS tracker that Michelle had placed in her possessions earlier that morning and it wasn't moving. It had accuracy to about six feet, so if she was sitting at her cousin's bedside and moving around his room, the tracker would not show movement. If only they could get word about Noah's condition, but they noticed no one wearing any kind of badge that said something in English. Everywhere they looked they were confronted with an alphabet they couldn't read.

"I don't see a reason to remain in China. There's something going on between the Chinese and Swiss pharmaceutical companies. However, we're not going to have evidence of any wrongdoing on the part of either company. Frankly, I wonder if the Chinese firm is going to buy the Swiss firm or even if they can or ever do something like that. If they are seeking a merger, does the

CIA care? Is there anyone that the CIA might charge with our attempted murder?" Jason asked. "Maybe I'm tired, but our role in China at the moment seems futile."

"Actually, I've felt pretty worthless here as well. Time to talk to Sheila to see if there is any more guidance. Let's take a taxi back to the hotel and see what the next steps are."

An hour later they were on an encrypted call with Sheila and one of her Chinese experts. They reported on what had happened and the fact that the U.S. still lacked evidence as to who caused the deaths of the American company employees. They had nothing to do with what was happening between the Chinese and the Swiss company, though they might want to alert their Swiss counterparts that something was up. Sheila had confirmation that the FBI and the SFPD still had no suspects but that the American company was safe. Eventually they reached a consensus that there was nothing more to do in China and so they booked their flight home for the next day. It was an unsatisfying conclusion, but the world had bigger problems at the moment.

Sheila planned on having a conversation with her Swiss counterparts and hopefully they would hear about what Noah's relationship was to the Chinese company and potentially get him some assistance with his injuries from his embassy.

Michelle and Jason had a quiet night and arrived at the airport for their departure early the next morning. They expected the usual airline and immigration routine for international travel and were surprised when they were sent to another room for further discussion. Their electronics and passports were removed by the officials who escorted them.

Michelle gave Jason a worried side-long glance, but he was his usual cool self. They sat at a table awaiting someone knowing that their passports were not in their possession. They looked around the room for cameras and then looked at their watches, starting to worry about boarding their plane on time. Michelle stood up and tried the door, but it was locked.

Then she tried to guess where the cameras were located and if it was possible that she could teleport them out of the room without being caught on camera.

Finally, she decided that some acting was required. "I wonder why we were directed here. If they hold us much longer, we're going to miss our flight. Do you think they'll pay our change fees for a new flight?"

"They should as they're the one making us late. I can't even check out when the next flight leaves as they took our cell phones. Maybe we should knock on the cameras to get their attention that we are running out of time."

"That's a good idea," she knocked on every piece of glass she found, saying, "Hello is anyone in there? We're going to be late for our flight!"

Still nothing happened, no one came in. Michelle grabbed a chair and stood on it repeating her early actions of knocking on any cameras. She wanted to hit them hard enough to break the lenses so she could take Jason and disappear. She knew that although her impulse was to teleport immediately, she couldn't show her skill on camera. Instead, she discovered she could bend the brackets and aim the camera elsewhere. As there was just the one camera at the ceiling, she decided that she would bend that, then stand to the side of the one-way glass and disappear. She leaned into Jason and whispered her plan. They had wisely kept their backpacks on their backs when they arrived in the room, and they had no idea where their luggage was located. Still, Michelle and Jason were worried about trackers being added to the packs. So, they decided to go to a place by the Pearl River and search for trackers.

Michelle stood on the chair and moved the camera and then they quickly moved out of the range of where they believed the second camera was located and Michelle teleported them to the riverbank. They did a quick search of their belongings and then each pulled out the stuff they wanted to keep and put it into a spare plastic bag that they kept for such purposes, and they threw what was left into the river to have the current take it away. They teleported home with the spare plastic bags tightly adhered to their bodies.

"Well, hopefully none of that was caught on any Chinese cameras. We had better call the boss. She'll want to kill our electronics that we had to leave behind."

They did and scheduled a meeting with her offsite as they weren't expected to arrive back in the United States until the next day. They met at a park to chat and walk. It was considerably colder in Langley than the sub-tropical climate of southeastern China. It was also about an hour before dusk compared to the early morning in China. They met on a path that was filled with trees begging to shed their fall foliage.

They recounted their tale and ended with, "Did we do the right thing, leaving when we did? Any thoughts as to why they were holding up our departure?" Jason asked.

"You've been back for about an hour, and I haven't had a call from my counterpart in China. We'll see if they eventually call. I hope you weren't caught on camera. If you were, I would say that you'll need plastic surgery to change your identity for your own safety," Sheila said, looking concerned for her agents. "At least any photo captured by the airport had a face that was already altered."

They walked in silence as it was clear that Sheila was thinking.

Finally, she spoke. "I think you made the right decision for Jason and the wrong decision for the agency."

"Explain," Jason said.

"We've lost other foreign agents to China. Despite being husband and wife, you would have likely been separated, and then it would have taken longer to find out where Jason was located. We would have spent months getting you home and you might have stood trial for trumped-up spying charges."

"You're saying you would rather have me rotting in a Chinese labor camp?" Jason asked.

"Yes, if it kept Michelle's identity and abilities safe. We can only hope that you did indeed block all of the interrogation room cameras before you left. As to whether there were trackers on your person at that time—we don't know if the Chinese were successful in planting them on you. I hope they're searching all over the Guangdong airport for you. I'd also like to see if we can list you aboard your flight from China so that it looks like someone screwed up in China."

"It's nice to know where I stand with the agency," Jason muttered.

"So why do you think we were detained?" Michelle asked.

"That is the eighty-thousand-dollar question. China has been known to detain visitors over real or imagined business or debt issues. Some visitors say it could take months to figure it out. They detain people from leaving, but don't necessarily lock them up while they slowly investigate. I wonder if the pharmaceutical company, or maybe Noah or Sabrina, filed a complaint with the government just to make your life difficult. It could be something as simple as that."

"I hope so. I hope they were going after us over an imagined slight rather than because they knew we were spies," Michelle said.

"You're not spies, you're case officers," Sheila said with a small smile. "We'll monitor their communications to see if we can understand what happened. I'll also make a note to myself not to send you to China."

"Well, we weren't making progress on the case, so I was ineffective in that country. However, in this country do we have any information on who murdered the lab employees? I think the Swiss company was behind it, but does the Justice Department have enough proof to extradite anyone from Switzerland or China in regard to the deaths?"

"Not that I've heard."

"So what's the game plan to keep the company safe going forward? They can't stay in hiding forever."

"Last I heard they had a mutually beneficial relationship with the National Institutes of Health. With the company leadership dead, the company employees have lost their will to be a tiny independent company. The Cancer Institute inside NIH is happy to have folded them into the family. I heard they have a big announcement coming in the next few days."

"So our role in this investigation sounds like it is at an end," Jason said.

"I think so. The company is carrying on and we've been unable to dig up any evidence of who the murderer was. The two deaths remain open cases for the FBI and SFPD."

"Okay, then we're on our own for a few days," Michelle said. "I'll head for California until you have a new mission for us."

"I do have a new mission for you, but since you're not arriving from China until tomorrow, I can't assign the mission to you until the following day. So the two of you need to be in my office at eight in the morning on Thursday. Understood?"

"Yes," they both responded, happy to have a few days off between cases.

They parted ways, splitting up to head to their respective homes. Michelle planned to check in with her children. If they had time, she would show them some of the magical skills at work in her small town. If they didn't have time, she would still spend some time at her second home. There was always something that needed to be done. She and Jason had been on this assignment for three weeks, spending time between San Francisco, China, Virginia, Russia, and Switzerland. It was a month since she had made it to her home in San Martin, California. She may as well continue to confuse her internal body clock.

She was able to arrange dinner with her kids before she headed back to Virginia. Ashley cooked a meal from scratch. Her kids wanted to know what she did for the agency, but case officers were sworn to secrecy, so she kept it brief.

"I've spent time in five countries and the only one I can tell you about is Iceland since that wasn't an assignment. I took my agency partner to Iceland so we could view the Northern Lights. I also saved the life of someone about to be run over by a subway train. That's all I can tell you."

"Wow, you live such an exciting and glamorous life. Can you teleport me to dinner in Paris at some point?" Ashley asked.

"Of course, dear. Just remember the time difference. Paris is nine hours ahead of California. So if I took you there right now, we would be searching for an all-night café at three in the morning."

Ashley looked at the timer on the baked chicken she had roasting in the oven. "I have about fifteen minutes right now. Can you take me to Paris for five minutes so I can see the Eiffel Tower lit up?"

Michelle paused to look up the Tower's hours and it was closed. That worked in her favor.

"Sure. Here is what we're going to do. I'm going to teleport us to one of the Eiffel Tower's walkways, that way I don't have to worry about landing on someone else on the ground. You can look at the view briefly, then we'll go to ground level wherever it is safe and then come back here."

They did just that and were back in five minutes.

"Mom, that was the coolest experience I've ever had. I'm so bummed I didn't know about this sooner and I'm so sorry we gave you grief when you first told us six years ago. Let me know when you have time off next, and I'll arrange that dinner in Paris."

"Okay, I can get all of you somewhere one at a time, but Sarah, I won't move you until you have the baby. I don't understand how my teleportation works, but I wouldn't risk your health or the baby's health on a whim."

"No worries, Mom, we agree with you. Once our child is old

enough to understand teleportation, we'll have to keep it a secret until they can also understand how to keep it a secret . . . probably not until they're a teenager. When they're an infant and toddler, it will be a blessing not to spend time on a plane with them. Just imagine saving us from the airport and a long time on a plane with an infant. That's a bigger gift than teleporting Ashley to Paris for dinner," Tyler said.

Ashley stuck her tongue out at her brother and then they proceeded with dinner. Michelle was renewed by the time spent with her children and was bright and cheery when she reported to Sheila's office the next day.

She smiled at Jason and said, "Good morning, everyone."

Sheila frowned at her and said, "I guess Miss Sunshine had a great day off."

"I did, thanks for asking. My daughter, Ashley, is an excellent cook. What did you do, Jason?"

"I just tried to figure out what time zone I was in," Jason said with a grin. "I'm not as young as I used to be and between placing trackers at night and being in too many countries, I slept the entire day away."

"Good for you! What's our next assignment, Boss?"

"I told you that our Russian agent whom you rescued regained consciousness. He relayed some information that made the agency nervous and might be related to your case in China. We need both of you in Russia to continue information gathering. Eric Karros was somehow exposed as working for the agency and it's no longer safe for him there. Also, he has quite a concussion with a prolonged recovery time. We have an appointment to talk with him in twenty minutes," Sheila said, looking at her watch and standing up. "Let's go."

They took separate cars to the hospital caring for the agent. He was pale with a bandage covering part of his head. The lighting was dimmed to lower the pain level of the agent's headache. Sheila performed introductions.

"Ms. Watson, I understand you managed to roll me out of the way of an incoming train and then managed to carry me over your shoulder out of the tunnel to a waiting CIA vehicle. Thank you for saving my life. You must do some exceptional weightlifting to have carried me out of there. Thanks."

Michelle wished Sheila had briefed her on the story they told Eric. She scrambled to reply, and in the end, said, "I had an adrenaline rush like lifting a car off someone. I couldn't do that in normal times, but the danger of the trains supercharged me. And you're welcome."

"Eric, you made contact with someone in the military, and I understand that contact believes that President Kozlov is planning some concerning activities with the military. Tell us about the rumors you've heard," Sheila asked.

"I've been working on an informant for nearly two years. The informant hasn't been happy with the direction that President Kozlov is taking the country. He has been especially unhappy once he started the war in Ukraine for many reasons, including that his son died due to poorly maintained equipment. Military leadership tried to tell Kozlov that they weren't ready to invade Ukraine, but he simply eliminated the leaders who told him that. Russia has reported some five-thousand troops dead, but experts think it might be closer to sixty-thousand soldiers. A lot of young men will never come home, and the military will not admit to their deaths. Still, my informant stayed in his military role with the hope that he would at some point impact the direction of the war."

"How did you stay in touch?" Jason asked.

"We left a group of rocks in a park in a certain pattern if he had information to pass on. If he did, then we would meet in the train station and ride the same subway car and he would leave me a note before he exited at a station. The secret police are everywhere and so we would plan to meet then cancel at the last moment if things looked dicey to either of us."

"How frequently did that happen?" Jason asked.

Eric thought about it for a while and replied, "Perhaps once a year."

"So you weren't worried about the informant canceling on you? What was your process for cancellations?"

"I was and I wasn't. He implied he had some good information for me which meant it was more than gossip. Our process was usually last minute. If either of us failed to show two minutes before the appointed time, then the meeting was off. He failed to show, so I knew I needed to get out of the station. The best way to do that is to board a subway car. I headed that way, but I thought perhaps I was being followed. I jumped aboard a car that was just about to leave and the person I thought was following me did also. I jumped out at the last minute, and he didn't. Once the train left the station, I went down into the tunnel where you found me."

"Okay, but I found you about four hours after you were supposed to check in. Were you just hanging out in the tunnel for hours?" Michelle asked.

Eric closed his eyes for a while. If they hadn't seen the frown lines on his forehead, they would have thought he was asleep. Then he opened his eyes and focused on them.

"I thought I saw someone else watching me intently, so I went down into the tunnel. I had explored it once before when I had night vision glasses. I didn't have them on me this time, so my plan was to make it slowly to the next station. But you saw the tunnel—progress is slow. Just about the time you get used to the dark, a train comes along and screws up your pupil size. And since I didn't have night-vision goggles with me, I had to move from alcove to alcove slowly. People leave you alone, but you have to stay away from the trains. Then I felt a terrible pain in my head and that's all I remember."

"Perhaps someone followed you into the tunnel? When I was down there searching for you, I had night-vision goggles on and I didn't see any violence on anyone other than you. I was grateful that I was able to move you out of the way of the train. Let me tell you, it was close. I can still feel the train bearing down on me."

"Once again, thank you for saving my life."

"I wish I had seen who hit you. I rescued you not knowing you were the agent we were looking for. It was only when I got back out to daylight that your face matched the photo of the person I was searching for. So there was a big piece of luck there. I just didn't want to see a human being crushed by a train."

"I'll say. The life of an agent is a dog-eat-dog world. I'm happy that you had the humanity to try and save a perfect stranger. When I recover from this concussion, I'd love to work with you again."

"I'll take note of that," Sheila said. "Do you have any idea what the information might be that the informant was going to try and pass on to you?"

"I think it was information about bombs that Russia planned to use."

"Nuclear bombs?" Sheila asked.

"I don't think so; I think it was more likely dirty bombs."

"Dirty, how?" Jason asked.

Some dirty bombs were filled with nails, and called dirty because shrapnel was released causing secondary damage. Sometimes "dirty" referred to the use of a radioactive isotope.

"I think Kozlov was thinking about putting nuclear waste in the bomb. It was also somehow connected to China. He didn't know if it was China's suggestion or if China was egging on Russia to be the bad guy on the world stage. My informant was trying to find the connection between the two countries."

"I thought you said it wasn't a nuclear bomb?" Sheila said. "I know China has nuclear weapons, but roughly ninety percent of the world's nuclear weapons are owned by the United States and Russia. Why would China be a strategic partner in this other than they don't like the United States?"

"Every major country in the world has medical waste that is radioactive, including Russia. Also, like the United States, they're running out of places to store this medical waste. I think Kozlov had this idea to kill two birds with one stone. He was going to solve the medical waste problem and at the same time inflict terrible and unpredictable harm on the Ukrainian army. I think China was just sitting on the sidelines trying to find out if it was a viable option. Rumor had it that a Chinese pharmaceutical company in conjunction with the state provided funding to Russia," Eric explained.

"Oh my gosh!" Michelle said. She had friends who went through cancer treatment and had radiation for their treatment. She could imagine the damage that kind of radioactive waste might do to the average Ukrainian citizen fighting the Russians.

"You should talk to that American company and find out if their breakthrough solution was going to reduce the amount of radioactive medical waste produced in cancer care. While that is great for cancer patients and the environment, it might put Russia's and China's strategies in regard to dirty bombs on the back burner. Maybe the Chinese pharmaceutical company wasn't worried about declining sales, but rather was influenced by the Chinese military being disappointed over the loss of radioactive medical waste," Jason said.

"Granted that's only if China and Russia move to this new cancer therapy and away from the old strategy that produces waste. From what I know about China, and it's admittedly little, I would think that China would move on to the new therapy, but Russia would stay lost in the past," Michelle said.

Eric had placed his hands on the sides of his head and he was rubbing his skull as if the speculation by Jason and Michelle hurt his head to understand.

"We're going to have to verify the validity of that intelligence. That would be a disaster if Russia carries through with that, let alone if China wants to fire dirty bombs on Taiwan. I'm going to start with doctors on this campus to understand what kind of harm that medical waste could inflict," Sheila said.

They could see the man in the bed was fading and his frown lines were back. Michelle said, "Eric, you look like you need to rest. I've had a concussion and it seems like the more you try to think, the more your head feels like it's in a vice. We'll come back later."

Sheila looked like she wanted to question her agent more, but studied him and had to agree with Michelle.

"Would you like us to darken the room more?"

"No, my eyes are closed," he said softly as though he was trying not to hurt his head with his voice.

They quietly left the room and headed to the parking lot. There were hospital staff around who didn't need to hear their conversation, and so they waited until they were outside to discuss what they heard.

CHAPTER 19

"Well, that's a scary idea. Do we know what the impact would be? Is medical waste a problem for the world?" Michelle asked.

"I don't know, and this is the second rumor I've heard about Kozlov doing that with bombs so we need to take this seriously," Sheila said.

"How would we even stop something like that? If you look at all the hospitals in the United States generating nuclear waste, where would you collect it from and does all waste created have an equal impact? Sounds like we need to talk to a nuclear physicist," Jason said.

"Yes. The agency has an expert that I will talk to, but the two of you should be prepared to head to Russia. Given the seriousness of this rumor, I'd like you to teleport between our two countries. I don't know if I'll be sending you back to Moscow or perhaps a place as cold as Siberia, so have winter clothing ready to go on a moment's notice."

"What about China?" Michelle asked. "Do we have any work to do there?"

"Not yet. I think they are content to watch Russia and see if they're successful with this idea. So not only do we need to stop Russia, we need to provide China with a reason not to go there themselves."

"And Switzerland?" Jason asked.

"I'm going to inform the Swiss government about Noah Schmidt. I find the Swiss to be very principled and I think they'll stop all activity including the sale of Noah's company to the Chinese. I predict based on my past interactions that Noah will find himself unemployed and cast off to another country. I don't see Noah being a threat."

Michelle and Jason nodded and left to prepare for the next mission. Sheila had her phone to her ear, probably arranging her talk with the nuclear physicist.

A few hours later, they had a better understanding of the story after another meeting with Sheila. The ability to do large-scale damage like the bomb that was dropped on Japan in World War II would not result from medical waste. The damage that would be done was more psychological and economic damage. People would panic and an area would have to be evacuated while scientists studied the degree of contamination. People might die from being trampled to death, but few, if any, would suffer acute radiation sickness. However, if a bomb was dropped in the right places, then the economic disruption would take years for a full recovery given people's rightful paranoia about radiation even in tiny amounts. It wouldn't be the hole in the ground or a few damaged buildings that they needed to worry about; rather, it was the desire not to live near an area of high radiation.

The Intelligence community strategized on what was the best way to handle the threat from Kozlov. He had not made any public threats. So they would start by trying to find the bomb building factory and examine the process. Sometimes a threat did more harm than the actual action that people were threatening. It was time for Michelle and Jason to scour Russia looking for the bomb building sites.

"This feels like our first case together when we were looking for a uranium enrichment lab," Michelle said.

"This is different in that the nuclear waste has already been created, and instead of storing it in a safe location while it slowly loses its radioactivity, our friend Kozlov wants to scare the bejeebers out of people and disperse it over a wide area. We know the waste is being created at major hospitals in Russia. We should start with hospitals in Moscow and St. Petersburg that offer nuclear medicine or radiation therapy and see if we can track what they are doing with the radioactive waste after it's been generated. Or if the CIA knows where exactly Russia builds its bombs we could start there," Jason said.

"There are sixteen cities with a population of over a million people and there are sixteen major hospitals in Moscow and St. Petersburg. So if we just stuck with Moscow, you'll have your hands full studying the hospitals there," Sheila said.

"Where do they manufacturer their bombs?" Jason asked, thinking this might be the shorter list of locations to examine.

"They have a few locations outside of, but close to, Moscow and we'll start there," Sheila said. "I'll give you maps and pictures, so you know what the weapons look like."

"Okay, but how do we tell if they have medical waste inside of them?" Michelle asked.

"I'll give you a Geiger counter which will pick up radioactive activity."

"Should we wear lead aprons to protect our health?" Jason asked.

With her grandchild in mind, Michelle looked worried too. If she was exposed to radioactive materials, she would need to stay away from her daughter-in-law and the new baby until she could be proven to be non-radioactive. It was amazing how a grandchild could change your way of thinking.

"I don't know. Teleporting with a lead apron on could be weird. The weight alone might throw off teleporting," Michelle said. "Get me some kind of a lead garment. By the way, when I mention a *garment*, I'm talking head to toe," Michelle said doing an internet search. She leaned over to Sheila with a picture of a full-body radiation protection suit.

"Got it?"

"Yes. Is it a condition of you traveling to Russia?"

"That and a Geiger counter. I didn't tell you, but I have my first grandchild on the way. I need to not die from radiation poisoning and I need to be safe to go near an infant in about six months."

"Congratulations Michelle! Even without a new grandchild, I would want you to stay safe on this and every mission. You are very important to the agency and this country, and I'd pull you and Jason from this assignment before I would put you in catastrophic danger. Radiation poisoning is an awful way to die, and we would never want to expose a case officer to that. We're dealing with a potential medical waste bomb release which is far less damaging, but the paranoia associated with the word *radiation* is bad and Kozlov is counting on that."

"Ahhh . . . you feel that way about me even though I never completed spy craft 101," Michelle said trying to lighten the mood.

"Yes, despite the fact you didn't complete the course," Sheila agreed and followed Michelle's lead to inject humor into a dangerous situation. "Seriously, though, I'm going to work on finding you protective supplies, so stay ready to go. Normally, I'd say, 'Stay at home with your cell phone on,' but with you two I can just say be ready to teleport back here at a moment's notice."

"I'd like to prepare for this situation more. Can you assign me to a Russian specialist who can teach me about the country and perhaps Kozlov's way of thinking?" Michelle asked.

"That's an excellent idea," Jason agreed.

"Yeah, I should have thought of that," Sheila said. "I'm used to you popping into countries on emergency missions, so you don't get the same briefing that most case officers get since you don't need it, but in this case, it may help you find what we're looking for. Just a moment and I'll arrange it," Sheila said, sticking her head outside to talk to her assistant.

"I asked Susan to send up our Russian specialists and book a conference room. We have different specialists on different aspects of Russia. You'll be hearing from our head analyst and our Russian military expert. I think they are the most critical. Susan will direct you to the conference room."

"Thanks," Michelle and Jason said.

They spent the remainder of the day talking with the analysts. They had clearance levels such that Michelle and Jason could talk openly about the purpose of their mission in Russia. They decided their first place to look was a missile factory northeast of Moscow in a city called Korolev. Their Russian military expert spoke with another analyst to understand how a missile might be constructed normally and then with a little radioactive medical waste.

"I assume the company would do tests on its missiles. Any thoughts as to where they might conduct those tests?" Jason asked.

"On empty land, and they have plenty. We'll check the satellites and see if we have anything going on. What would you do with that information?" the military analyst asked.

"Good question. I'd say we would take a Geiger counter and see if there's radiation, but that might be detrimental to our health. Besides, are there even roads near where the explosions are taking place? Still, it would be interesting. If we could get close and send a Geiger counter in on a drone, that would tell us something," Jason said.

"Yeah, I like that suggestion, Jason," Michelle said.

"It's not easy to sneak a drone into Russia, so you may want to rethink that plan."

"Actually, based on the map you have here, we'll cross the border from Finland and that way we can carry what we need,"

Jason said. "The two of us are pretty awesome at taking up residency in countries that we shouldn't enter."

They walked away from the meeting with a list of missile and bomb manufacturers as well as test sites. Next, Sheila arranged a meeting with a nuclear scientist to help them understand how radioactive medical waste could be weaponized.

From talking with all the experts, they had an understanding about how Russia would make these dirty bombs, where they would test them, and what they would do with the bombs. It was likely that they planned to bomb Ukraine, but Kozlov seemed off his rocker and therefore he was unpredictable in his thinking. If he really wanted to, he could move bombs to Siberia in western Russia. Alaska was only fifty-five miles from Russia and certainly within striking distance.

The final part of the plan was figuring out how they would get radiation suits and Geiger counters to the various places inside Russia that they needed to inspect. Also, given that winter was arriving, they needed some warm Russian-looking clothing. They were provided with pictures of the Russian winter garb they should wear so as to not attract attention. The nice thing about winter was they could hide so much under a beat-up parka with a hood.

Michelle practiced teleporting around with the extra gear and lead suits and found she had no difficulty other than her balance. They had a list of about ten locations to check, and she and Jason were ready for the first locations they needed to explore. They also debated whether to go to these sites in the day or at night. In the bigger cities, they opted for the day and in the isolated areas of Russia, they opted for nighttime exploration.

CHAPTER 20

"Ready?" Michelle asked Jason.

He nodded and she wrapped her arms and one leg around his bulky body. He did likewise. In the blink of an eye, they were in a location at night in Siberia. They went from the beginnings of sweat in their bulky clothes to having their eyes water in the cold. They looked around and were glad to see not another human in sight. This was an area where missiles were detonated. They pulled out their Geiger counters from the backpack and using GPS walked toward a hole in the ground identified by the CIA's satellites. The counters registered radiation despite the fact they were still a half-mile away from where the missile exploded. Fortunately, the agency set them up with very sensitive counters and it was not a dangerous level in the least. They continued their hike over the uneven snowy surface toward the coordinates. The radiation level increased, but still not to a concerning amount. The ground naturally had radiation from the sun and other sources like uranium and cobalt that might be naturally occurring in this part of Russia. All they knew was they were in no danger with the radiation level reading on their Geiger counter.

"Dang, it's cold here. My hands are freezing while holding on to this meter."

"Yeah, I have to blink frequently in case my eyeballs freeze. Perhaps we should have added goggles to our equipment. Especially night-vision as we could walk faster and not freeze our eyeballs."

"I could take us back to get more equipment."

"No, we'll get through tonight. We've got more places to explore in these conditions, so we'll be better prepared next time. I'd rather hurry because we don't want to be noticed and frankly, I'm worried about them testing another missile while we're here. The military expert indicated they like to target the same hole, so we need to listen for that sound overhead," Jason said.

"My Geiger counter is now increasing as we get closer to the target. I wonder if we're seeing the natural radiation of this area, or are we walking on an area that has had prior rocket tests explode on it?"

Jason was about to respond when they heard a sound. They both looked around them and Michelle said, "Mark where we are coordinate wise, and then let's get out of here for about five minutes."

Jason nodded and marked their location. The sound was getting louder and they could see a light coming their way. It looked like it would target them, but the area was so vast that it was probably targeting the hole they were looking for as it was just about a quarter mile ahead. However, given their body heat they didn't want to chance that they might make the missile move off course. Jason moved into position and they soon were in Michelle's condo, which felt overheated in their gear and with the buzz of adrenaline.

"Let's get our night-vision gear and head back in about five minutes," she said, setting her watch's timer.

She teleported Jason to his apartment so he could grab his night-vision goggles and they watched the timer. They both put their goggles on and hugged each other in teleportation mode and were soon back on the Russian snowy field. They listened for a moment and looked at the sky and saw another missile heading their way, and so they teleported back to her condo.

"Should I set the timer for thirty minutes or should we just go to another location?" Michelle asked her partner.

"Let's try another location as we're all geared up. Perhaps by the time we're done with the next location, we'll be able to go back. I don't think they can afford to waste rockets all night."

"Yeah. Okay."

They looked at the list and pictures where Michelle needed to teleport them. She had them at a new location that was as quiet and dark as the first one had been before the Russians started firing missiles. Again they had their Geiger counters out as they approached another hole in the ground that might contain medical radioactive waste. The Geiger counter level of radiation increased as they got closer to the target. It wasn't at all at a dangerous level, but it was more than the naturally occurring level of radiation. The night continued to remain quiet. It was just them and the snowy landscape.

"This is such a barren area. I would be depressed living here given the short days and the cold," Michelle said.

"Apparently it's not that barren," Jason said, pointing to some light in the distance that seemed to be coming closer. They stopped and listened, trying to determine what it might be. It wasn't in the sky so no need to worry about a missile, but was it someone on foot, in a vehicle, or riding some kind of animal suitable to this cold place? They stood in silence watching the approaching light.

"Duh, let me teleport closer and see what it is. I'll be back in a sec." Michelle said, teleporting away from Jason. He stood in place waiting for her return. A moment later she was back.

"It's a slow-moving vehicle. Apparently, we're walking on a frozen river and in the winter time you can drive over it in a vehicle. It doesn't appear to be a military or even company vehicle. I think it's just a random Russian driving around in the wintertime. When the vehicle gets closer, I'll teleport us out of the way briefly while it passes. How much farther do you think we have to walk to the location? I know I could get us there faster by teleporting, but I want to make sure we don't land in an area of high radioactivity. At least by walking there, we'll hopefully see a gradual increase in radioactivity."

"Perhaps another quarter mile in the direction of that vehicle. It seems weird that it might drive right over the previous site that might have been a missile-testing site."

"Russia doesn't have a long history of caring about the health of their citizens. It wouldn't surprise me that they didn't notify the residents in this area of the country that they may get exposed to excessive radiation or perhaps might drive their vehicle into a ditch because they didn't know a missile previously blew up the ground. All they probably can see is endless frozen tundra. They don't know how firm that snow is, and after enough of it falling, the snow might fill in any divots."

They continued to move toward their GPS coordinates while the vehicle continued to move toward them. Michelle looked around to find a convenient place to take her and Jason and saw a tree in the distance. It was all they needed—just a single tree to hide the fact that there were two people out in the middle of nowhere, Siberia Russia. They waited twenty minutes to make sure the vehicle cleared the area that they were exploring and Michelle teleported them back. They looked around for the vehicle once they arrived at the location and were happy to see that the darkness likely hid them from any mirrors on the vehicle. Their Geiger counters continued to have climbing radiation levels, but still it was nothing to worry about. They reached the site and according to what the nuclear expert had explained to them back in Washington, medical waste had not exploded here in a rocket. There simply wasn't enough radiation. With that, they returned to Michelle's condo for no other reason than to use the bathroom before returning to the area that seemed to have active missiles.

With their bladders taken care of, they returned to the first site. They stayed hugging each other while they made sure that they were in no immediate danger. All was quiet, so they looked around for sound or lights coming their way, but there was nothing but the dead and cold silence of the Siberian fall.

"We seem to be safe. Let's hustle to where those rockets were hitting and see what we find," Jason said.

They pulled out their Geiger counters and proceeded in the direction that they had decided on before they saw the rockets hitting in the same general vicinity. Like the other sites, the radiation level began to climb. They got nearly to the edge of a hole before the Geiger counter read enough for them to be concerned.

They had a sample kit—a lead-lined bag to put a mixture of snow and dirt and whatever was making the Geiger counter unhappy. Michelle took the first one to Virginia and then came back for Jason and the second bag. They ended up in her condo and contacted Sheila to see if her office was clear for Michelle to drop off the samples. It was, and Michelle made two trips to drop off the boxes. Even though her teleportation process was instantaneous, she still didn't want two bags of radioactive dirt next to her body. She thought she should give thought as to how Sheila would explain the samples in her office and decided she didn't need to waste any brainpower. Sheila could figure out the answer to that question. They had more sites to survey that night and she needed to get back to her condo to knock off the next location on the list of Russian rocket sites.

They were able to eliminate the remainder of the nighttime sites in the next two hours. Their Geiger counters did not go off the rest of the night; they came home and got some sleep before tackling the remaining five locations in daylight. Three of the sites were going to be tricky. They were manufacturing plants of Russian missiles. The CIA expected them to be well guarded.

Somewhat rested, and minus the lead suits, they set off for the missile manufacturing facilities just north of Moscow. First they needed to take in the lay of the land. What was the visible security around the plant? The CIA had been unable to provide a blueprint of what the facility looked like on the interior, so the safest thing for Michelle to do was to teleport to the roof. From there, she could get a little picture in her mind of how the manufacturing facility was laid out. When she finished studying the roofs of the huge facility, she teleported back to Jason to discuss her findings.

She sketched out her vague design of the factory. They decided to observe the factory at all hours of the day and night for a few days to see if it had three shifts. It would be much easier to move around the building if workers were not there.

After observing the factory for several days, they had the routine down. The plant did not have employees between midnight and six in the morning, so that was when Michelle and Jason would explore the factory. If she found a safe teleporting space, she would return to Jason's side to bring him inside the building with her. If not, or if she teleported next to some kind of night security guard, she would handle the exploration by herself.

Unfortunately, her first attempt went badly. She teleported about five feet in front of someone. She disappeared as fast as she appeared and hoped, given the time of the night, that the person just decided his eyes were playing tricks on him. She then teleported to a different part of the factory. She had better luck the second time as it was dark and no one was in sight. She returned to Jason's side; they both grabbed night-vision goggles, and she teleported them back in less than twenty seconds. The hallway was still clear when they arrived, and they set about exploring the factory

Neither of them knew much about making rockets, and the area they were in appeared to be the manufacturing area for the people that made the wiring for the rocket. They were blinded when the lights were thrown on and quickly removed their goggles. It was another security patrol, and they could only hope they hadn't been seen before they ducked under a table while removing the goggles.

They heard a voice speak in Russian, but he was too far away for their translator app to hear the words and translate what he said. He began to walk around the room. Michelle and Jason debated whether they should leave or wait for the guard to leave. This felt like a routine patrol of the factory and perhaps a way for the security people to stay awake at night. They both found niches to tuck themselves away in and watched as the guard walked by, holding their breath. He continued on and ten minutes later, turned the lights off and left.

"Well, shall we continue exploring this factory or head back home?" Michelle whispered.

"Let's stay here. Unfortunately, I don't think there's anything helpful in this room. The wiring on a rocket would be the same whether it was filled with medical waste or not. We need to find a room where the rockets are assembled."

Michelle nodded. "Should I teleport us to another location, or should we walk there?"

"Let's try walking there. If we come across someone and can't hide our presence, then we need to teleport out and I will move close to you to do just that. However, if the security guard is like the one who just came to this room and we can hide, we should continue our exploration. Agreed?"

"Yeah. You're better at this covert stuff than I am, so I'll follow you. Let me try one more thing before we go. I'm going to wrap myself around your back and I want you to move your arms backwards around me, and let's see if that works for a teleport position. I'm just going to try and move us five feet."

It was helpful to know that they could teleport in this physical position. If they had to move fast, their positioning became critical. It worked, and so Michelle had one more tool in her teleportation toolbox.

Jason slowly opened the door of the room. They were in the hallway where the guard had entered. The hallway was dark, and so he whispered to Michelle, "It appears that the path is clear, but we're vulnerable in that hallway if a guard comes along and turns the lights on. Where do we wanna go from here?"

Michelle thought for a while about what she had learned surveying the company from the roof.

"I'm guessing that the missile assembly area is the largest room or building in this facility. My sense is that it is down the hall and to the right. I think it's a completely separate building, but there should be a hallway connecting these buildings. If the lights go on, then I'll grab you from behind and take you back to the room we came from. I don't see any way to hide from anyone coming down the hallway other than to get out of the hallway and I don't know what's behind all these doors and don't want to waste the time exploring. Agree?"

Jason nodded, and they proceeded forward, following her directions to where the missiles were likely manufactured. They traveled through several dark hallways with Jason in the lead before they came upon the building that Michelle thought was large enough to assemble the missiles. They had managed to escape detection from the security crew up to that point.

They approached the door to what Michelle thought was a big room based on the map in her mind of the missile-making complex. Jason pulled on the door, and it was locked. He pointed to the bottom as he took his goggles off. The next room had the lights on. Jason had a series of lock picks on him, and he tried to unlock the door. Michelle had seen him do this before and he could be as quick as ten seconds and as long as ten minutes. While Michelle could have teleported inside the room, with the lights on an unknown number of people might be inside and the last thing she wanted to do was teleport inside a circle of ten people which the room might contain if it was where the security force took its breaks.

Just as he seemed to unlock the door. It opened from the inside. Jason and Michelle were face-to-face with a Russian guard who raised his gun to point at them. She debated and then discarded the idea of teleporting them out of the situation as she had no idea what would happen if the guard fired a bullet before their earthy bodies were completely absent from the room.

She almost said "shit," but silenced her mouth at the last moment. That one word would give away their identity as Americans and Michelle's eyes were wide as though she were a deer caught in the headlights. In her five years as a CIA case officer, she had never been caught by the enemy while she was doing something. She waited for Jason to take the lead.

The guard said something to them in Russian and pulled up a walkie-talkie from his holster. He then clipped the speaker and spoke. Michelle teleported behind him and whacked him over the head with a stick that she had carried for this exact purpose. As the guard crumpled to the ground, she moved next to Jason and teleported them back to Virginia.

"Rats, it's going to be hard to get back into that company. They know they had intruders, and the intruders are gone. Fortunately, we didn't say anything, so there's no telling what country we hail from," Jason said.

"In my five years with the agency, this was the first time that I've been caught by the enemy. If we had it to do all over, again, should I have not teleported behind him, knocked his lights off, and brought us back to Virginia?"

"I think this might have been your only opportunity to teleport outside of the eyesight of the Russians. Now the problem is, that it's going to be much more difficult to explore that factory," Jason said. "With the guard's concussion, they have evidence that someone was there. That can't be a figment of his nighttime imagination."

"Yeah, I thought about that, but now that we know they don't operate around the clock, we can go back in the dark. I think this would be better if I went by myself, because I can get out of there fast. So fast that the security guys are probably thinking I'm a figment of the imagination, which is what I want."

"Of course, the guard had a quick look at you tonight, so you'll want a wildly different appearance the next time you visit that factory. I think in tonight's scenario, you had to waste time getting close to me, so we could get out of there safely. I also think that with the Russians alerted to our snooping, they might potentially post a guard in there around the clock. Regardless, you're going to have to teleport into the room, duck as fast as you can, and make up your mind as to whether you're being observed. If you aren't, you can look at those missiles. The question is whether you should go back tonight or wait a night. I guess that's a Sheila question. We better contact her."

Once they brought Sheila up to speed on the night's events, she agreed that Michelle should explore the factory by herself with Jason checking in with her frequently. Given the time difference, they decided to call it a day and grab some sleep before exploring the factory and the other sites on the list.

CHAPTER 21

By the end of the week, they had explored everything on their list and brought back two additional samples of dirt and snow that appeared radioactive. It was a low amount, but there was no reason for there to be any radioactivity unless it was a naturally occurring quirk of the soil or a rocket with radioactive waste recently hit the ground.

It was time for Michelle to go back to the rocket factory. She was dressed all in black, had black grease paint on her face, wore a parka and her quietest sneakers, and had a camera ready to take photos. She debated taking the Geiger counter and decided it was somewhat bulky, so she left it behind. If something looked potentially like radioactive waste, then she would make a separate trip back with the Geiger counter to measure the situation.

A different team at the CIA was investigating where the Russians were targeting the bomb with the medical waste in the rocket. Russia had a variety of rockets that could reach almost anywhere in the world. If they loaded the rockets aboard one of their ships or submarines, that gave them even greater range.

A lot of discussions were going on at the agency that Jason and Michelle were not privy to, for which they were grateful. It was far better to catch up on a good book in your condo, than listen to experts talk about countries they haven't visited while a plan is devised for the case officers.

The international community planned to put pressure on Russia by discussing their findings at the United Nations. Russia, of course, denied the findings and said any evidence was just a set up by the United States.

The agency was at a standstill on what to do with the situation. Having a medical waste bomb wasn't the end of the world. Likely more people would die from hysteria than from radiation sickness. Furthermore, China was sitting in the wings and the U.S. needed the idea to fail in Russia. They needed to do something and so the discussions, continued on what they should do.

The government decision makers weighted the pros and cons of range of options varied from blowing up the rocket factory to trying to find the sources of medical radioactive waste and bombing those hospitals so that the Russians suffered from the hysteria, and any fallout from the medical radiation waste. Jason and Michelle quietly waited for their agency and the government to make up their mind on what they wanted to do.

If they tried to block the waste at its source, then innocent Russian citizens would be hurt. If they blew up the rocket facility, Russia might be able to rebuild quickly and retaliate. In the end, the agency decided it needed to do a little more research. How was the radioactive medical waste reaching the rocket facility? Had it been stored in the wasteland of Siberia only to be collected by the Russian military for use? Or were hospitals ordered to send their barrels of medical radiation waste to a new location? It was going to require some new sleuthing.

The agency researched where the largest number of cancer patients were treated in Russian hospitals. Radioactive medical waste was also generated by nuclear medicine procedures, as well as computerized tomography, which was a type of x-ray, but the quantity was minor compared to the large amount that was generated through radiation medicine. Some radioactive waste was stored outside of hospitals as the radioactivity declined and then it could be poured down a sink after two months with some isotopes. Still, the agency decided that even mildly radioactive waste had the capacity to psychologically damage residents beyond the initial rocket strike.

The agency also did some research on Russia and interviewed a few physicians in the United States who had trained in Russia so they might understand what the waste process was. Their knowledge was out of date, so the agency gained no new information from that process.

Russian analysts determined there were two major hospitals in Moscow that provided radiation therapy, one in Saint Petersburg and one in Novosibirsk for a total of four major radioactive waste production sites. The plan was for Michelle to plant cameras that would record what happened to the waste inside the hospital and which way it traveled once it was sent to a disposal site. It was nerve-racking work for her as it was riskier than her prior work for the agency. Still, she couldn't think of a safe way for Jason to assist her, so tag, she was it. She was given pictures of medical waste collection containers and a pocket full of GPS trackers for her to place to give her spy agency the ability to follow the waste.

After the agency analyzed the movement of radioactive waste, she would have to go back and add street cameras to the top of a few buildings. These cameras would verify the data from the GPS trackers as further proof for the international community of Russia's activity of sending medical waste to a rocket factory. She didn't have any close calls with hospital staff nor on the rooftops. People weren't interested in enjoying the fresh air in the wintertime, particularly on top of a tall building. Once the case was over, she would return and remove the cameras so the Russians wouldn't find them come summertime next year.

The cameras showed them the path of the radioactive waste. They developed a plan for Michelle and Jason to momentarily delay the movement of the radioactive waste so they could add something. They could create a delay by damaging a couple of bridges, but that seemed like an obvious activity by the United States. They needed something less evident and spoke with some physicists about how they could nullify the radioactive waste. What would be a way to make it unusable for the rockets? Could they add something to the waste so that it would detonate upon launch rather than exploding at the targeted location? The scientists went to work modifying current explosives to meet the needs of this scenario. The substance needed to blow up upon ignition of the rocket, but not blow up as the waste was being delivered to the rocket factory.

The scientists needed to worry about their agent's safety and how they would get the substance to Russia and not have it explode in transport. When they thought they had a solution, Michelle and Jason asked them to demonstrate it. It was better if they had confidence that they weren't going to be detonated while taking the substance into Russia. They also wanted to make sure that if they had the opportunity to dump it on a cart going along the hospital corridor, that hospital corridor wouldn't blow up if the cart hit a bump in the floor, or even as it bumped along a road in the back of a vehicle. They watched from a distance at Langley as the agency scientists demonstrated the safety of their solution.

The next thing they had to understand before they traveled to Russia was how was the radioactive waste loaded into the rocket. The waste was stored in steel drums that looked too big to fit inside a rocket. Was Russia removing the waste from the drum and putting it inside a smaller container? What could they learn from the soil and snow samples Michelle had collected from Siberia?

The agency sent her back to Russia to track the radioactive waste drum once it reached the rocket factory to investigate what happened. The tracker showed the drum entering the facility and staying in a room for an hour or two before it moved back outside. Surely, they weren't pouring the waste into the rocket—that strategy would be extremely unsafe for the employees. Through cameras placed in the rocket factory room, it became clear that Russia had changed its waste container recently. There were new steel-looking canisters inside the drums. The canisters were lead lined and placed directly into the rocket. The cameras showed the workers removing the warhead and replacing it with the medical waste canister. While the rocket wouldn't detonate on impact without a load of explosives in the warhead of the rocket, it would hit the ground with enough force to break the canister open and release the medical waste.

Some government scientists developed a liquid they could add to the medical waste and it would explode upon the massive vibration and heat generated by a rocket when it launched. The question was, how did they secretly intercept the medical waste so they could add their substance? Now that they knew the lid was removed from the drum and individual canisters removed and loaded into the rocket, they needed a way to reach inside the steel drum. Did they attempt to do it at the four hospitals, or did they attempt it at the rocket factory?

Michelle and Jason had also been learning Russian so they could speak a few sentences that would be enough for them to do what they needed to do. Thanks to the GPS trackers and cameras, they knew about what time of day the hospital department moved the radioactive waste to the loading dock to be picked up. The plan was for Jason to stop the employee who was pushing the cart and move their attention away from it while Michelle dumped the explosive substance onto the radioactive waste container. Jason would ask the employee where something was and speak a combination of languages enough to confuse the employee, while showing that person pictures of what he wanted. It wasn't unheard of for a foreigner to be hospitalized in Russia either because they were vacationing there or because Russia provided better medical care for the citizens of Iraq or Venezuela or Cuba than their own in-country services. Jason was by far the better actor than Michelle, so he would be having the fake conversation. Armed with the new knowledge of the canisters, they needed a new plan. A simple distraction wouldn't do.

The scientists created a product that was odorless, so Michelle didn't have to worry about the employee suddenly noticing a scent in the hallway. Fortunately, she only had to put about ten drops of the substance on the container of radioactive medical waste. Kudos to the scientists for figuring out all of these properties that made Michelle and Jason's lives easier as case officers in a hostile country.

Also, they picked a hallway that was poorly traveled by other people. The agency analysts learned this from studying the footage of the cameras that Michelle had placed around the interior of the hospitals.

After several days of observation, they noticed there was a moment where the employee moving the drums pushed the cart into the hallway, then returned inside on some kind of errand that took about two minutes before he returned to the cart. In that time, Jason stood in front of the door so the man would run into him. In Virginia, Michelle practiced taking the lid off and placing the requisite drops on the canisters contained within before they left. She now did her task under the pressure of discovery. They teleported out of the hallway before the employee returned. Whatever this employee was doing was also policy at the other locations and everyone breathed a sigh of relief when the drops were placed.

They were hearing from Russian sources and seeing satellite pictures of the exploding rockets. Eventually, the Russians admitted to the problem and, of course, blamed the United States, while never mentioning the fact that the rocket was going to carry radioactive medical waste. President Kozlov was seen with an eye patch after that first launch amid speculation that he had suffered some injury while observing the rocket malfunction. Those rockets were more psychological warfare than chemical warfare. They would have made places uninhabitable for months until nuclear experts declared the areas safe, and then would the citizenry believe such a declaration?

When the rockets exploded on the launchpad, they damaged it, and so Russia couldn't use the launchpads until they rebuilt them. Thus, the CIA wouldn't have to worry about the problem for at least another six months. It was unclear if Russia had discovered how the Americans sabotaged their radioactive medical waste terrorism plan. The agency would keep an eye on them in the long term to see if they would set up the system again, but at least they had a solution if they did so. All was quiet in China as well as they apparently made the decision not to follow in Russian footsteps. The agency heard little about Noah Schmid though there was an announcement of the acquisition of Noah's Swiss company by another company in Basel.

Michelle and Jason had a few weeks of vacation and so she made some plans with her children and brought Jason with her for a few of the activities. Of course, this was after they were checked by their agency experts to make sure they had no radioactive damage. The dirt and snow samples they had returned with were back from the lab with an analysis and they contained typical radiation medicine agents and posed no harm to them given the protective gear they had worn to collect the samples. The world was a safer place thanks to Michele Watson and Jason Smith. The unsung heroes were honored in a private meeting with the President of the United States, where they were given the Distinguished Intelligence Cross for their last three assignments saving millions of people around the world.

The End

Now You Don't See Me

Where Did She Go?

How Did She Get There?

<u>Dog Humor</u>

Eat, Play, Poop: Letters to my parents from camp

<u>New Urban Fantasy Series - Stephanie Jones</u>

The Awakening at Lake Tahoe (short story)

Witch's Medicine (2024)

ABOUT THE AUTHOR

I reside in Northern California with my rescue dog and cat. I love to travel, play sports, read, and drink wine and beer. I enjoy the diversity of the world and I'm always watching people and events for story ideas. All of my stories are generated by my imagination, I don't use AI to write books.

If you would like to sign up for my bi-weekly blog and announcement of new books, please follow this link: https://www.AlecPecheBooks.com

While you're waiting for the next story, if you would be so kind as to leave a review for this book, that would be great. I appreciate all the feedback and support. Reviews buoy my spirits and stoke the fires of creativity.

Readers that sign up for my blog receive a free prequel novelette for the Jill Quint Series.